TIME BLASTERS
BACK TO THE ICE AGE

Librarian Reviewer
Katharine Kan
Graphic novel reviewer and Library Consultant, Panama City, FL
MLS in Library and Information Studies, University of Hawaii at
Manoa, HI

Reading Consultant
Elizabeth Stedem
Educator/Consultant, Colorado Springs, CO
MA in Elementary Education, University of Denver, CO

STONE ARCH BOOKS
Minneapolis   San Diego

Graphic Sparks are published by Stone Arch Books
151 Good Counsel Drive, P.O. Box 669
Mankato, Minnesota 56002
www.stonearchbooks.com

Library of Congress Cataloging-in-Publication Data
Nickel, Scott.
    Back to the Ice Age / by Scott Nickel; illustrated by Enrique Corts.
    p. cm. — (Graphic Sparks—Time Blasters)
    ISBN 978-1-4342-0450-9 (library binding)
    ISBN 978-1-4342-0500-1 (paperback)
    1. Graphic novels. I. Corts, Enrique. II. Title.
PN6727.B544B33 2008
741.5'973—dc22   2007031251

Summary: David is stuck with the world's worst babysitter. But when she accidentally zaps
herself back in time, his problems are far from over. If she's still missing when his parents
get back, they'll freak out! David and his best friend, Ben, must blast into the past to save
the stranded sitter.

Art Director: Heather Kindseth
Graphic Designer: Brann Garvey

1 2 3 4 5 6 13 12 11 10 09 08

Printed in the United States of America

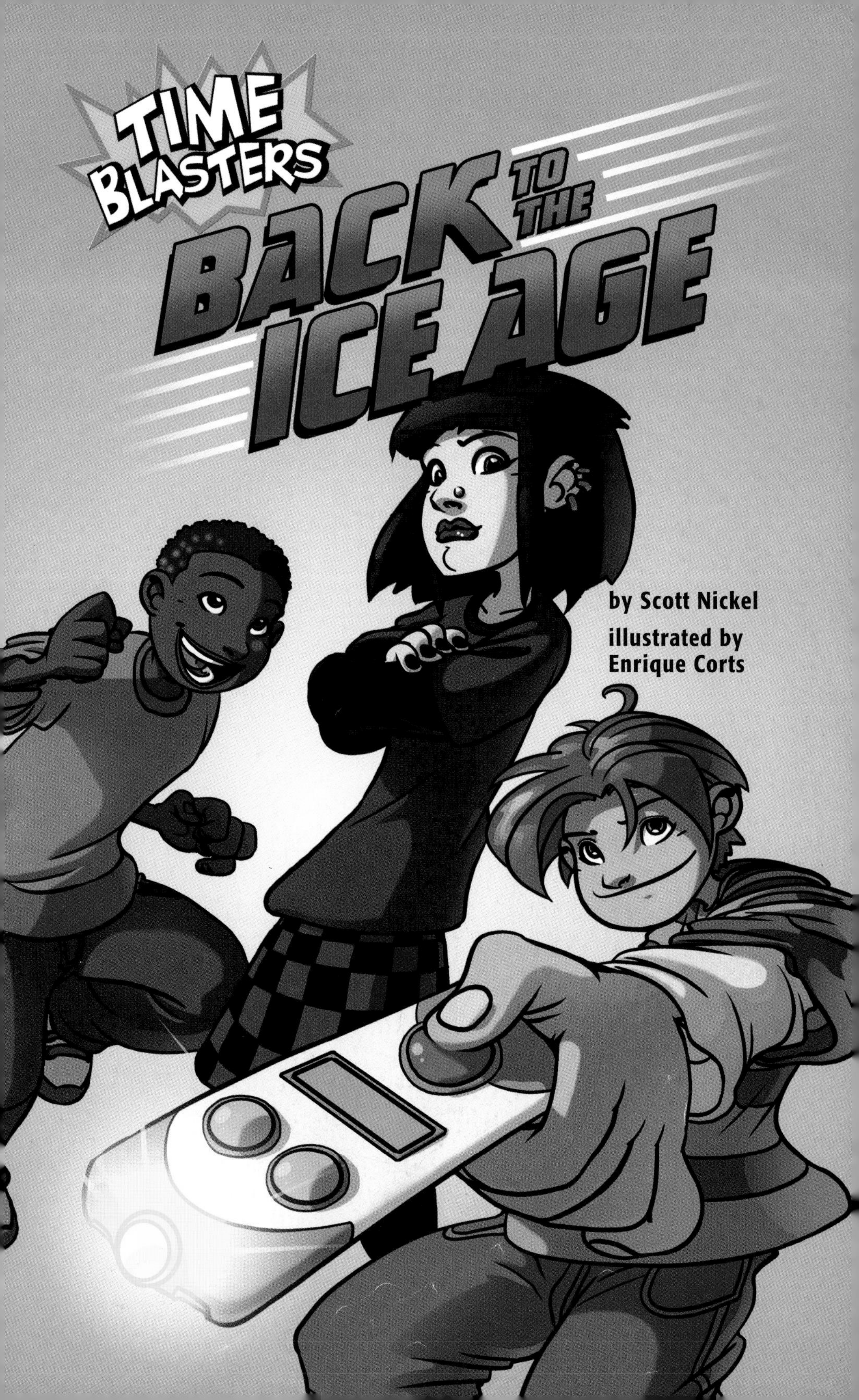
TIME BLASTERS
BACK TO THE ICE AGE
by Scott Nickel
illustrated by Enrique Corts

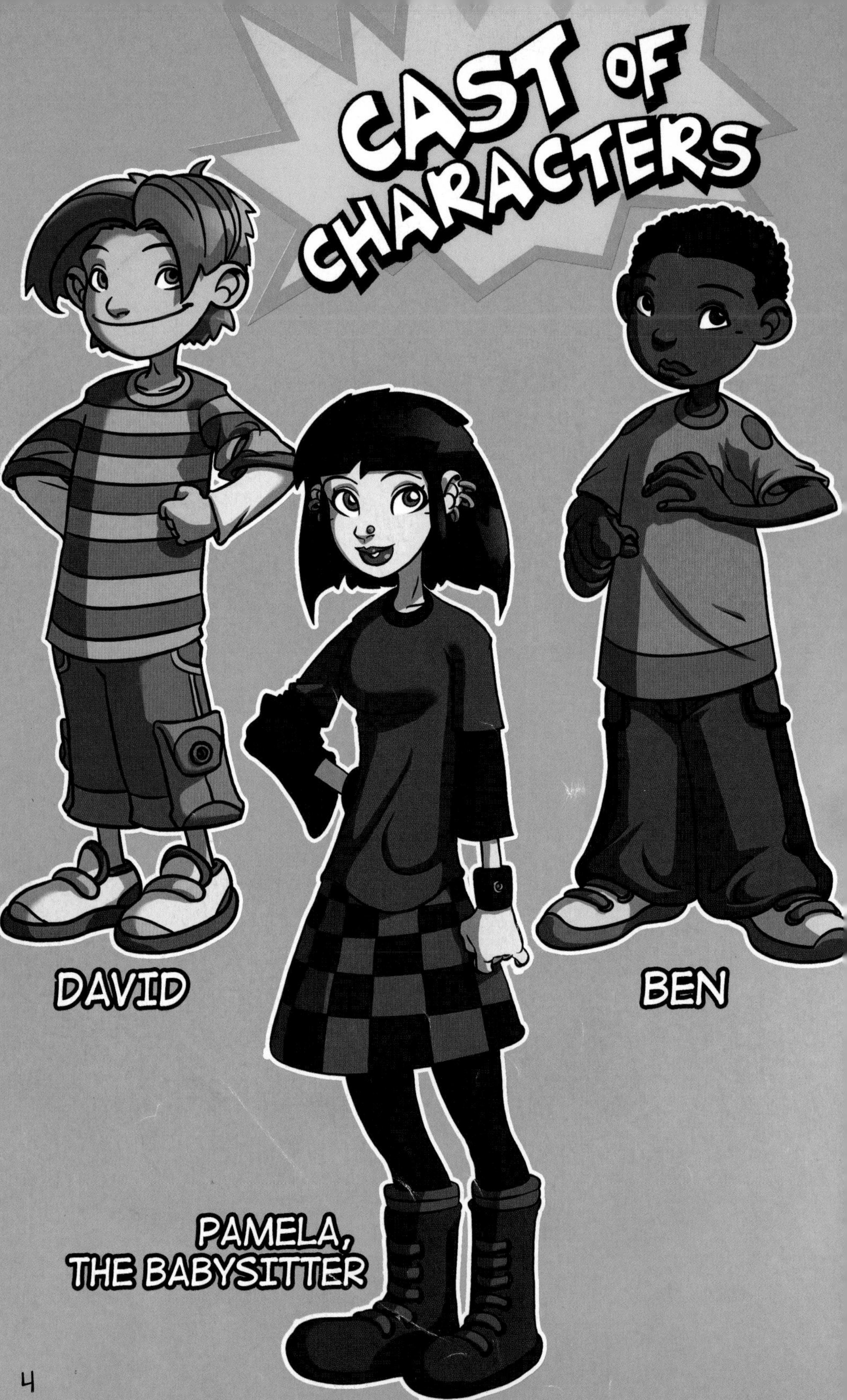
CAST OF CHARACTERS
DAVID
BEN
PAMELA, THE BABYSITTER

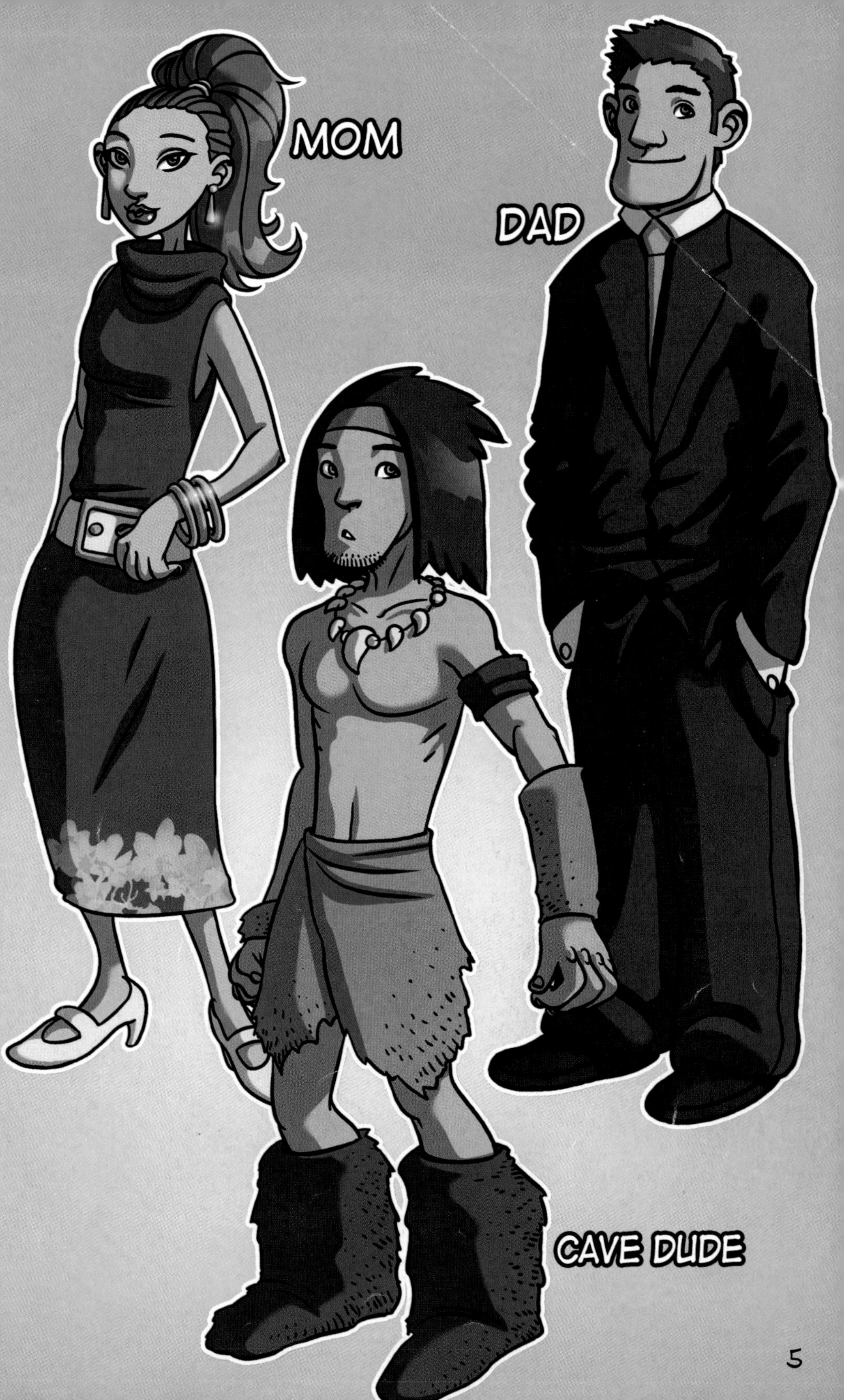
MOM
DAD
CAVE DUDE

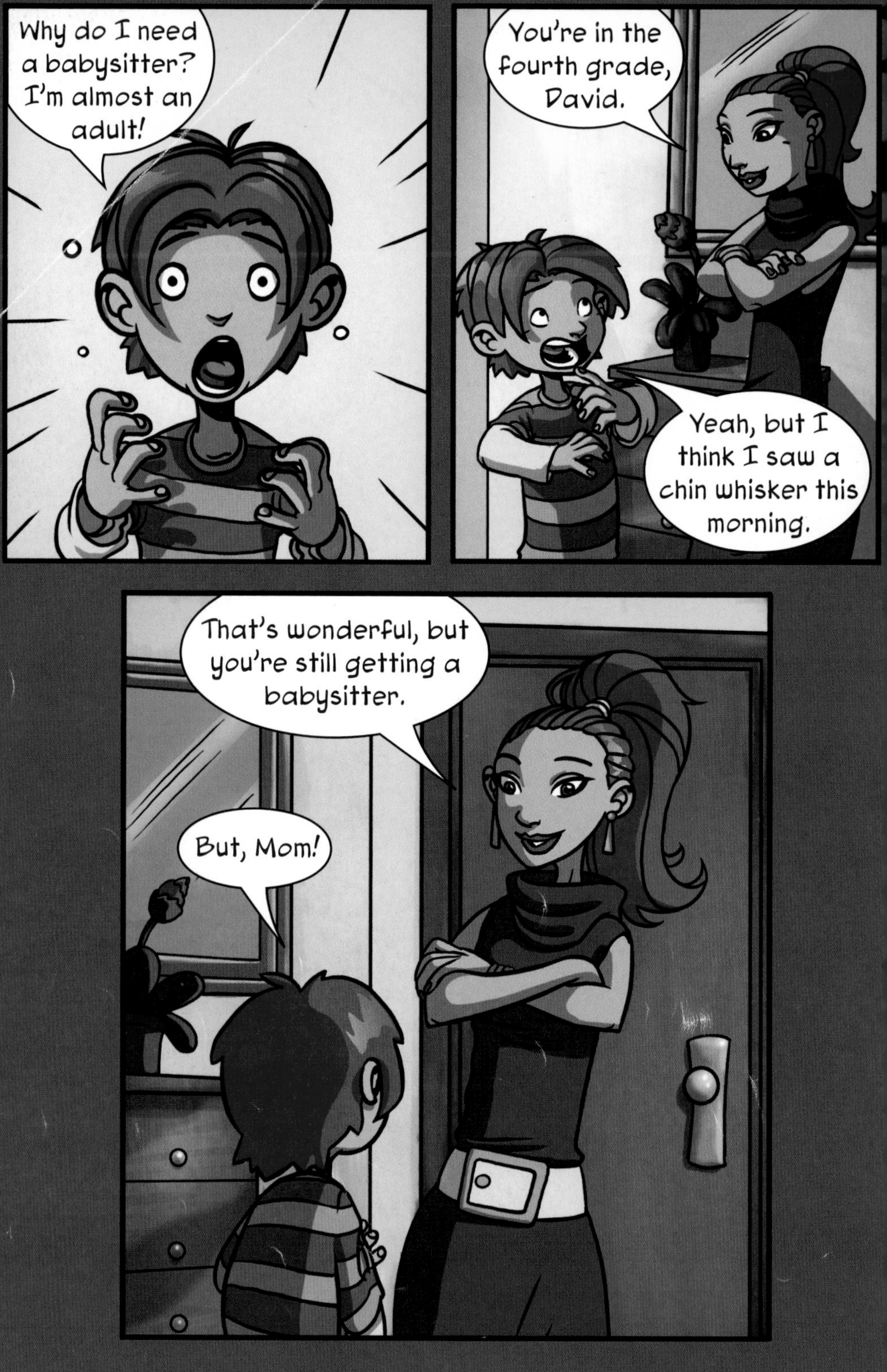
Why do I need a babysitter? I'm almost an adult!
You're in the fourth grade, David.
Yeah, but I think I saw a chin whisker this morning.
That's wonderful, but you're still getting a babysitter.
But, Mom!

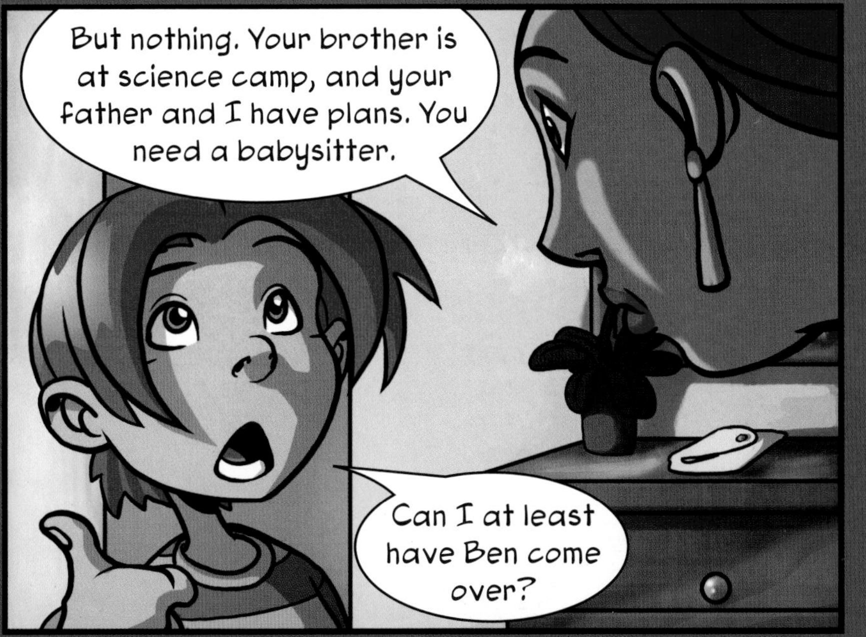
But nothing. Your brother is at science camp, and your father and I have plans. You need a babysitter.
Can I at least have Ben come over?

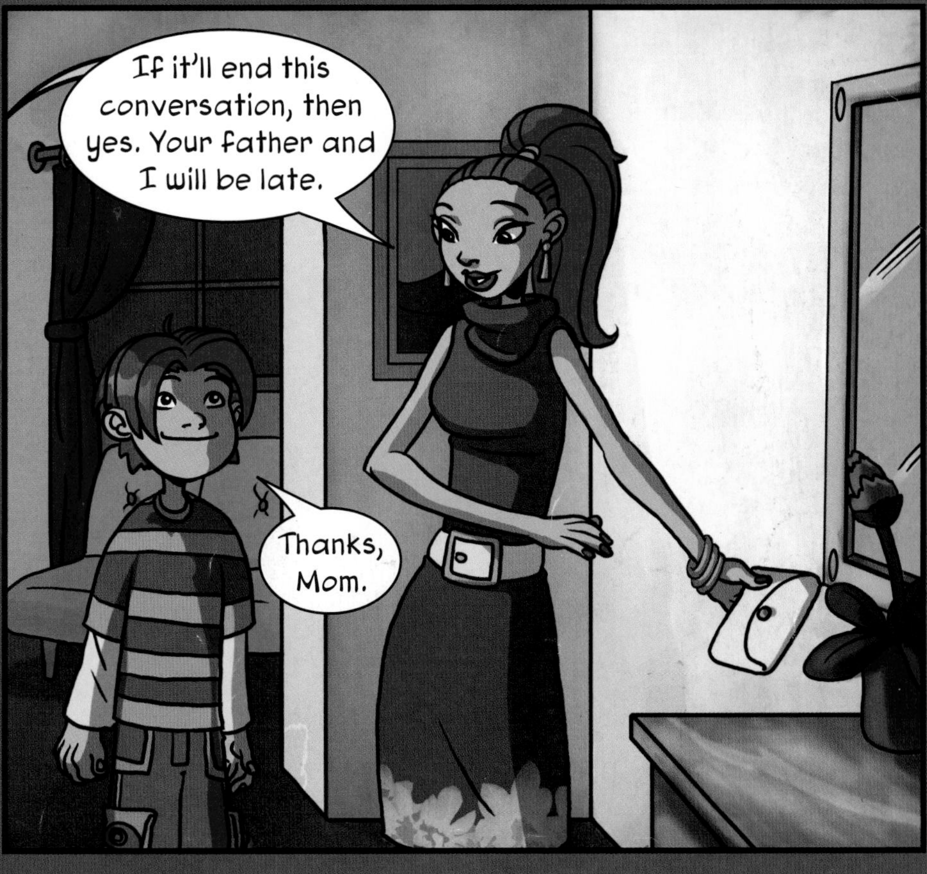
If it'll end this conversation, then yes. Your father and I will be late.
Thanks, Mom.

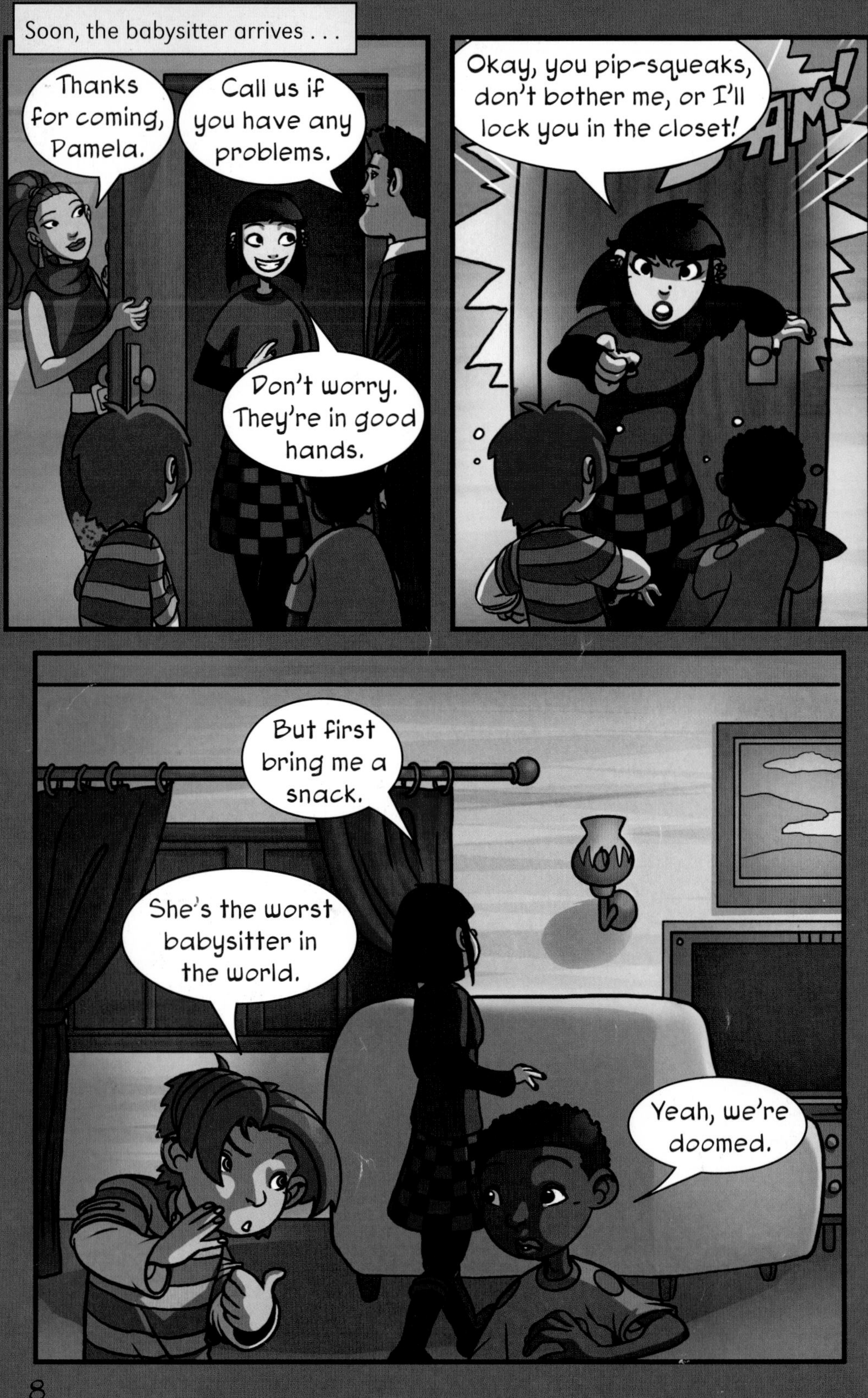
Soon, the babysitter arrives . . .
Thanks for coming, Pamela.
Call us if you have any problems.
Don't worry. They're in good hands.
Okay, you pip-squeaks, don't bother me, or I'll lock you in the closet!
SLAM!
But first bring me a snack.
She's the worst babysitter in the world.
Yeah, we're doomed.

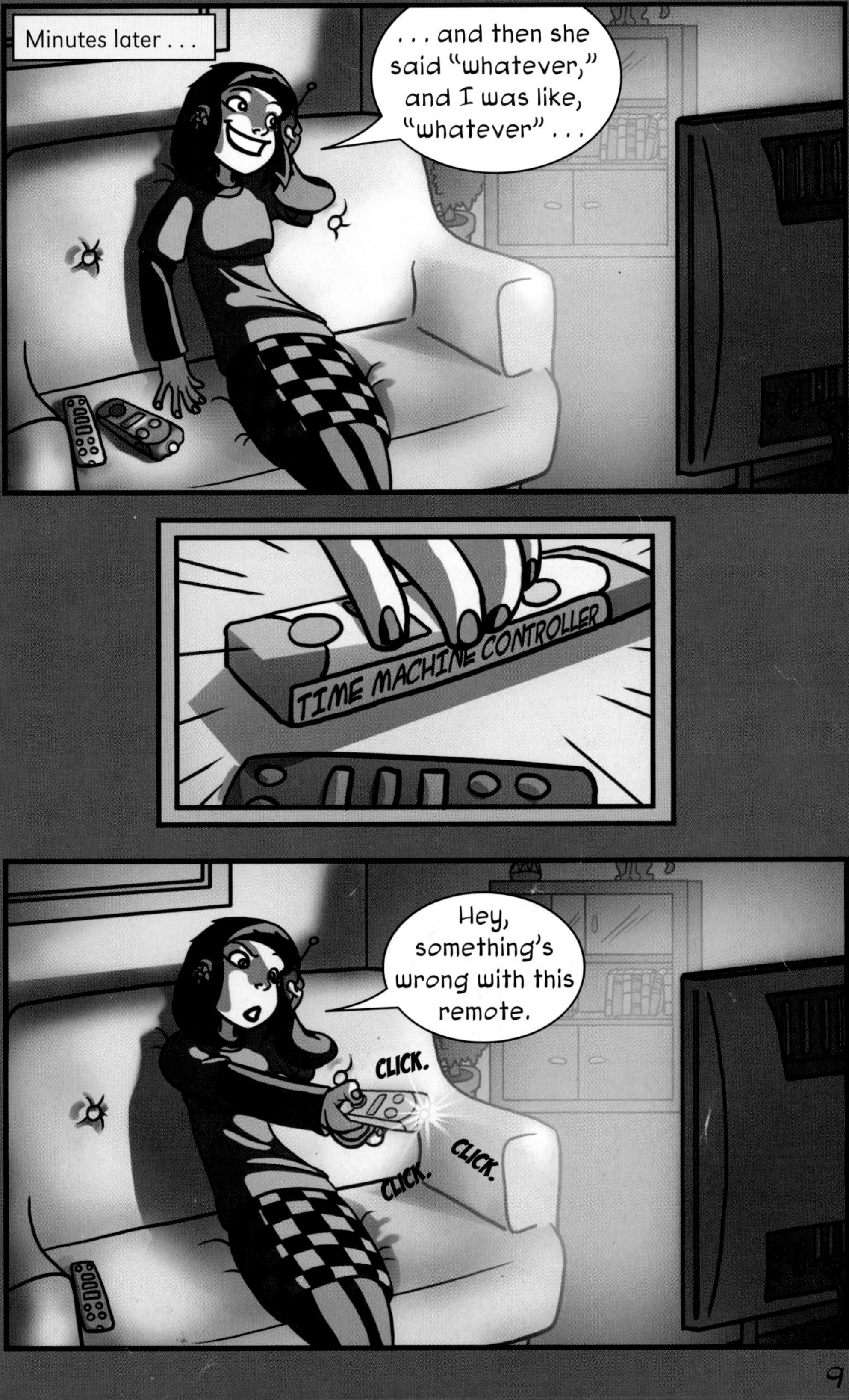
Minutes later . . .
. . . and then she said "whatever," and I was like, "whatever" . . .
TIME MACHINE CONTROLLER
Hey, something's wrong with this remote.
CLICK.
CLICK.
CLICK.

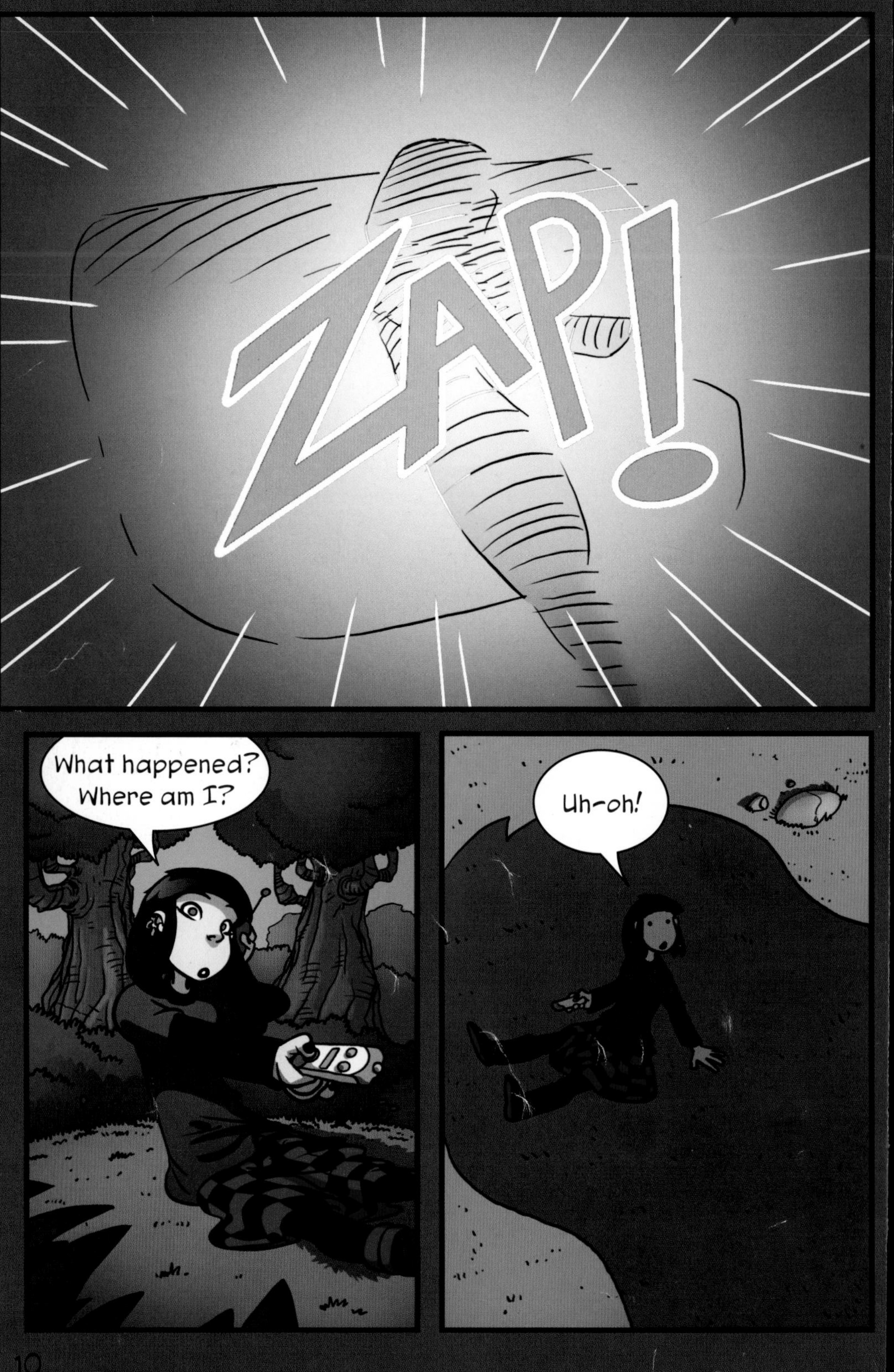
ZAP!
What happened? Where am I?
Uh-oh!

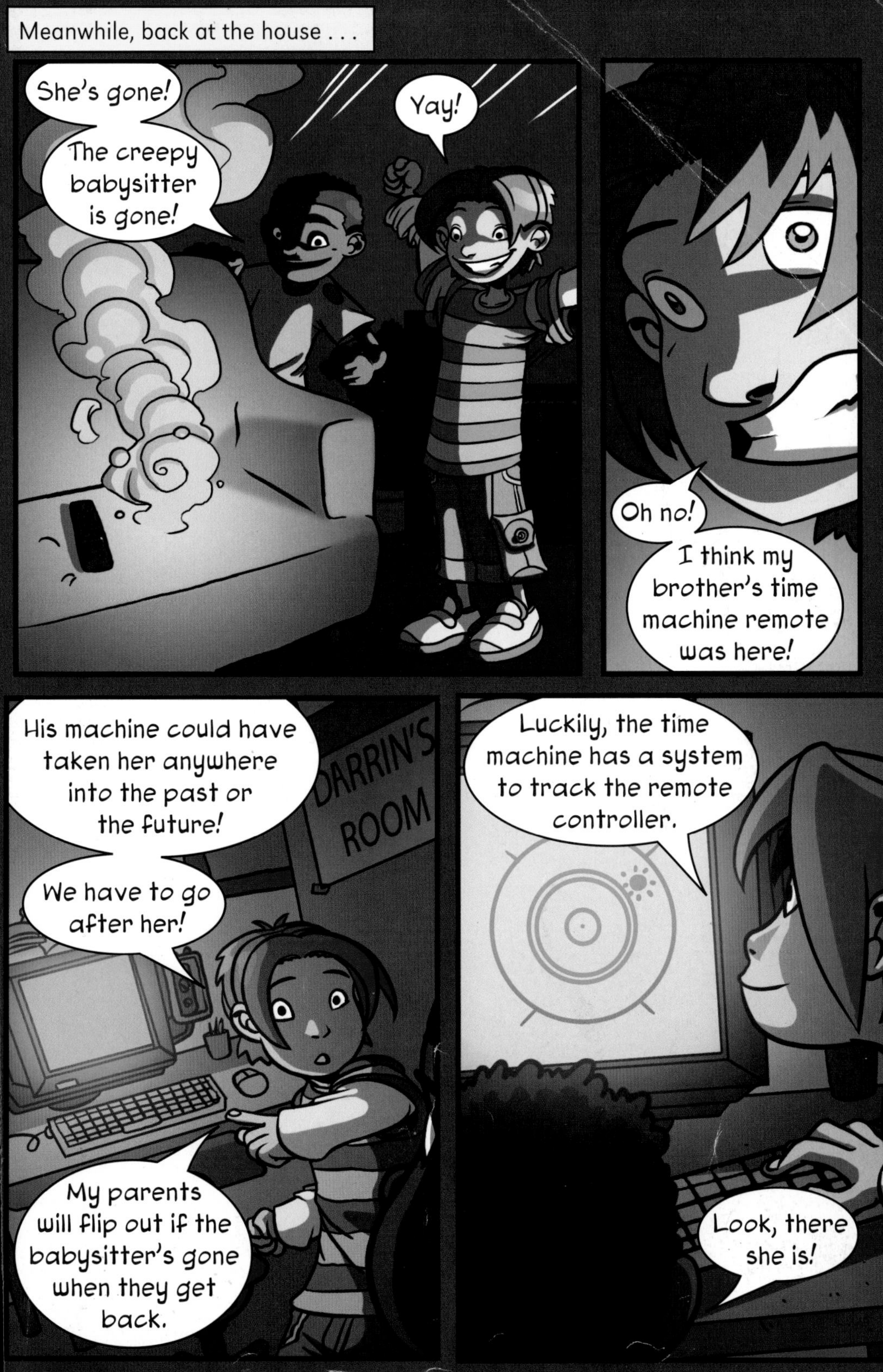
Meanwhile, back at the house . . .
She's gone!
The creepy babysitter is gone!
Yay!
Oh no!
I think my brother's time machine remote was here!
His machine could have taken her anywhere into the past or the future!
We have to go after her!
DARRIN'S ROOM
My parents will flip out if the babysitter's gone when they get back.
Luckily, the time machine has a system to track the remote controller.
Look, there she is!

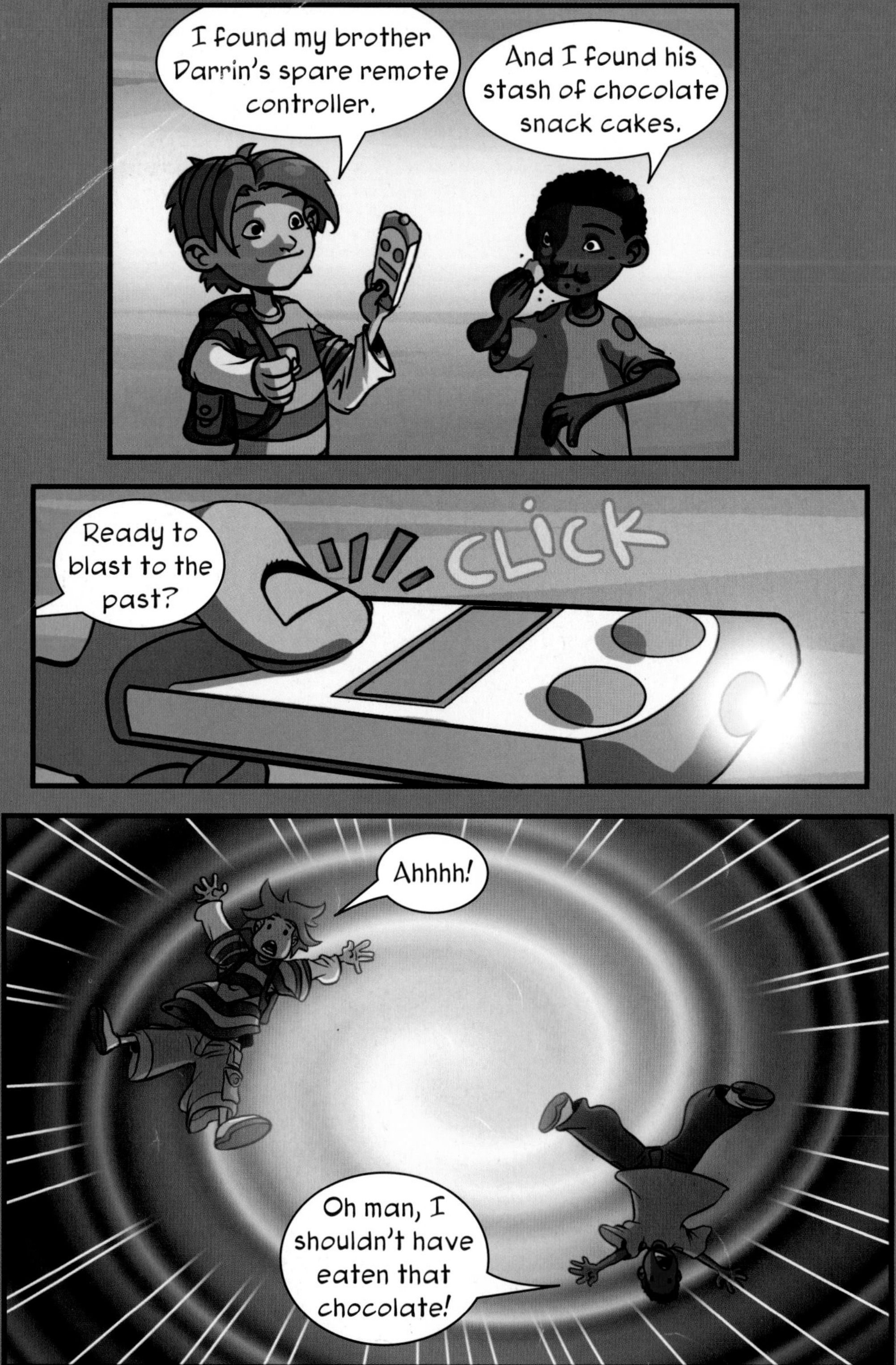
I found my brother Darrin's spare remote controller.
And I found his stash of chocolate snack cakes.
Ready to blast to the past?
CLICK
Ahhhh!
Oh man, I shouldn't have eaten that chocolate!

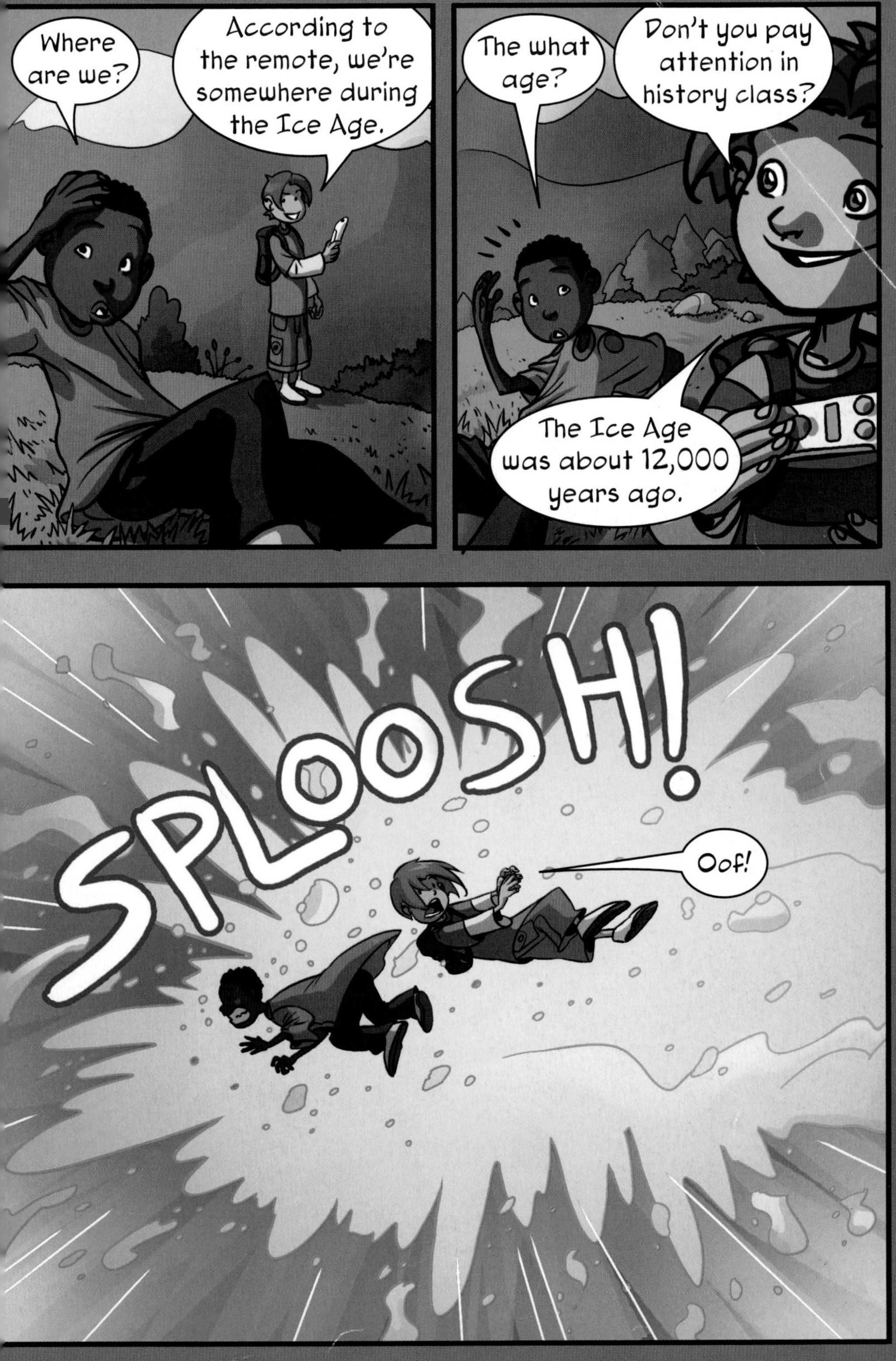
Where are we?
According to the remote, we're somewhere during the Ice Age.
The what age?
Don't you pay attention in history class?
The Ice Age was about 12,000 years ago.
SPLOOSH!
Oof!

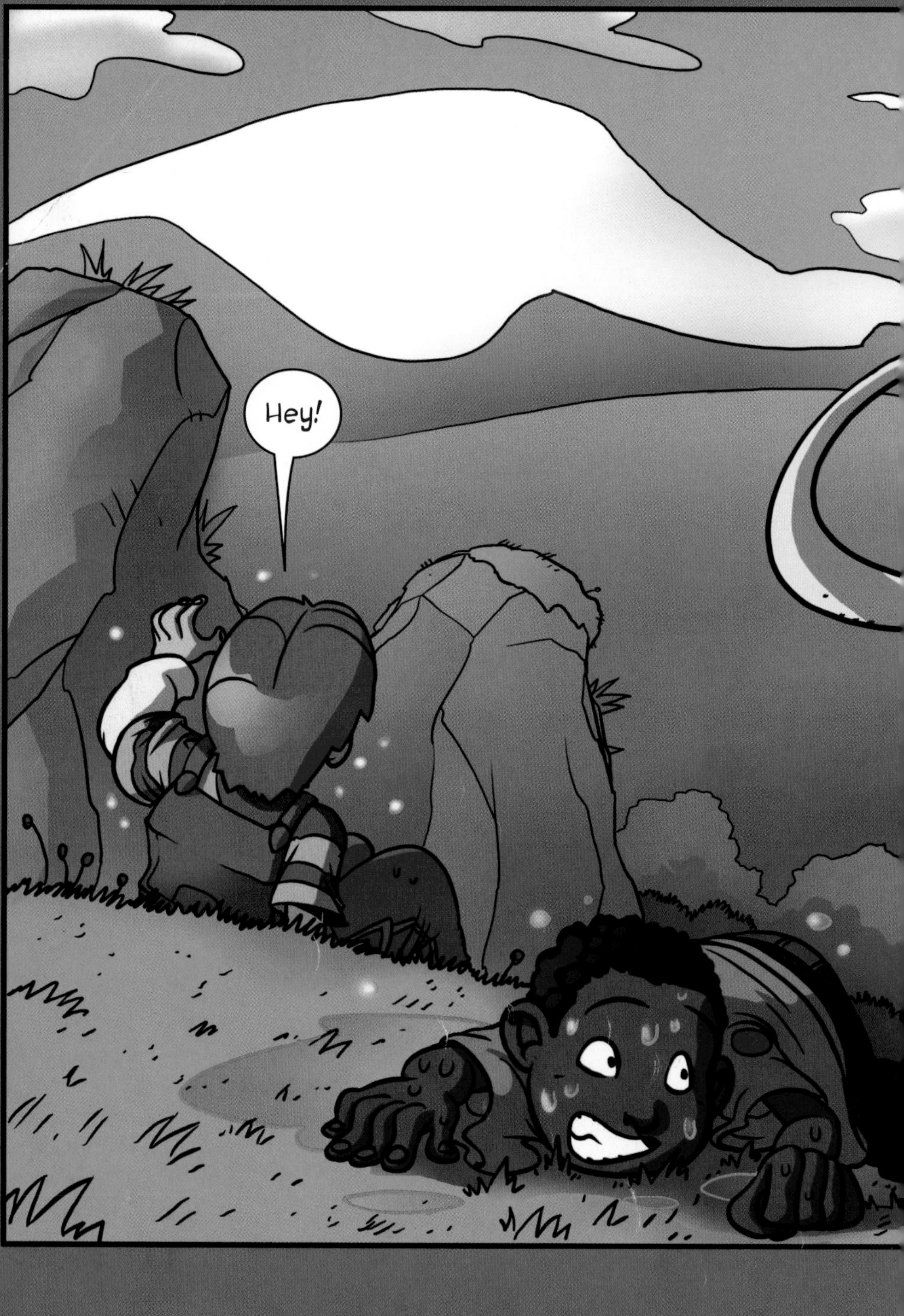
Hey!

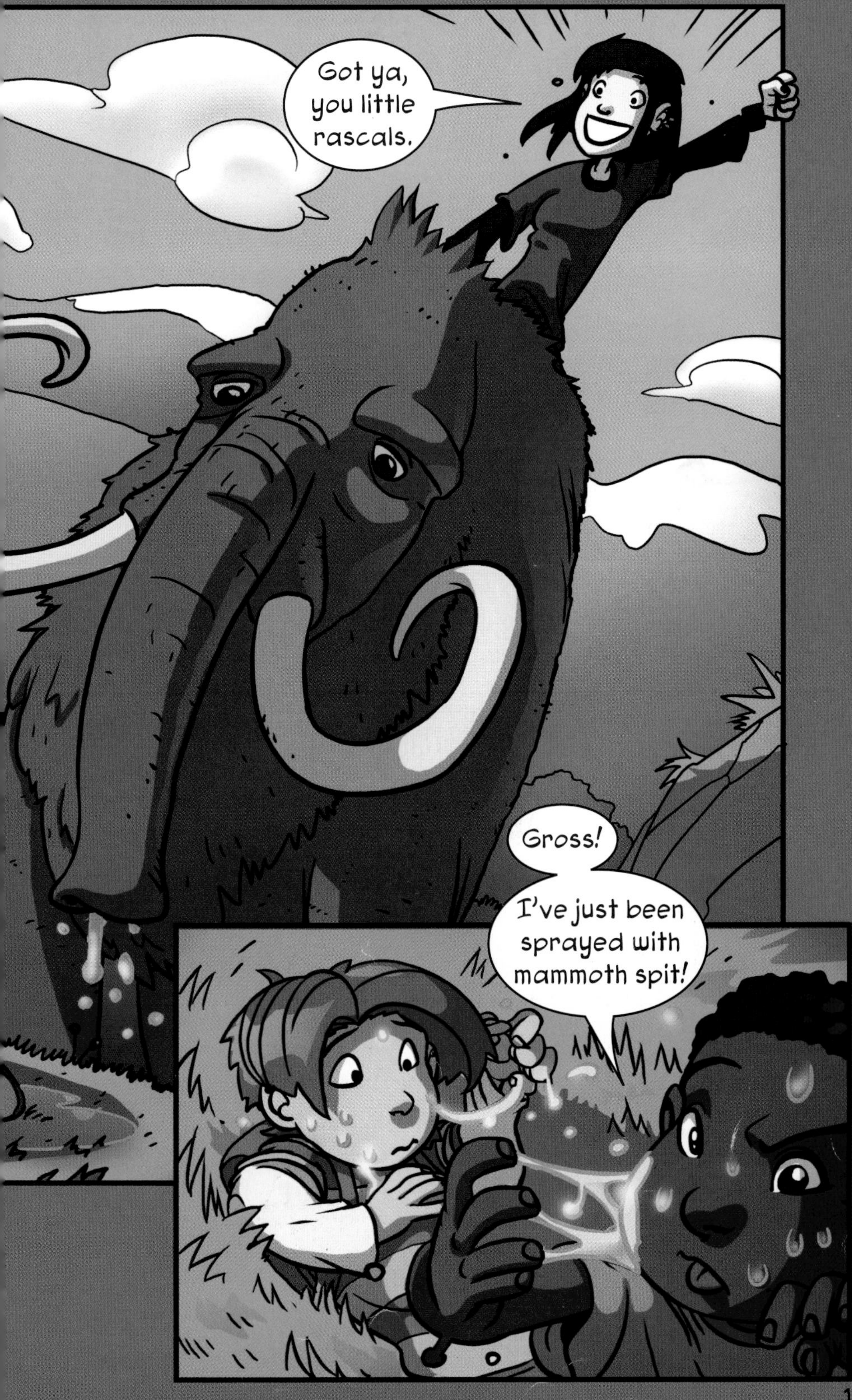
Got ya, you little rascals.
Gross!
I've just been sprayed with mammoth spit!

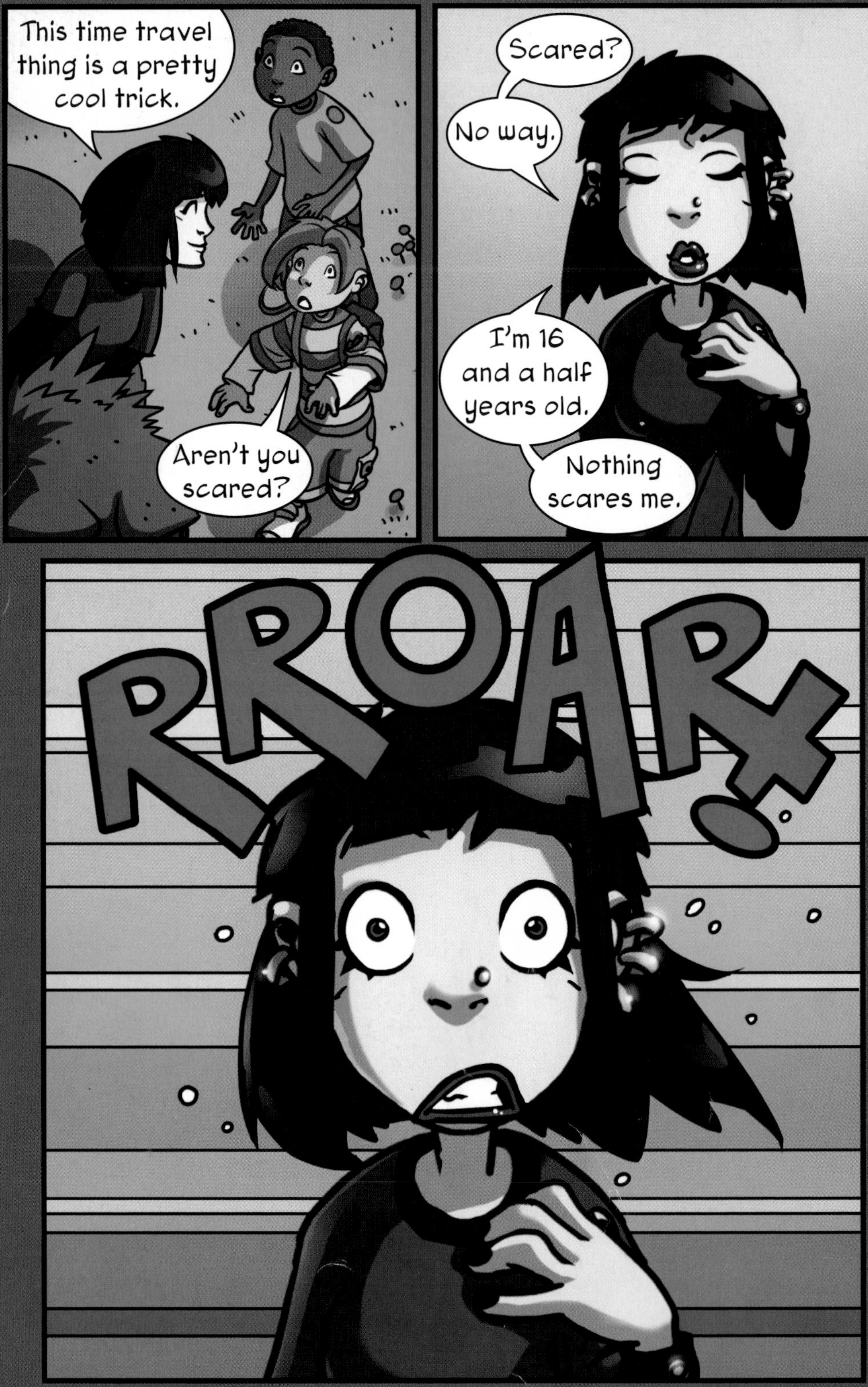
This time travel thing is a pretty cool trick.
Aren't you scared?
Scared?
No way.
I'm 16 and a half years old.
Nothing scares me.
RROAR!

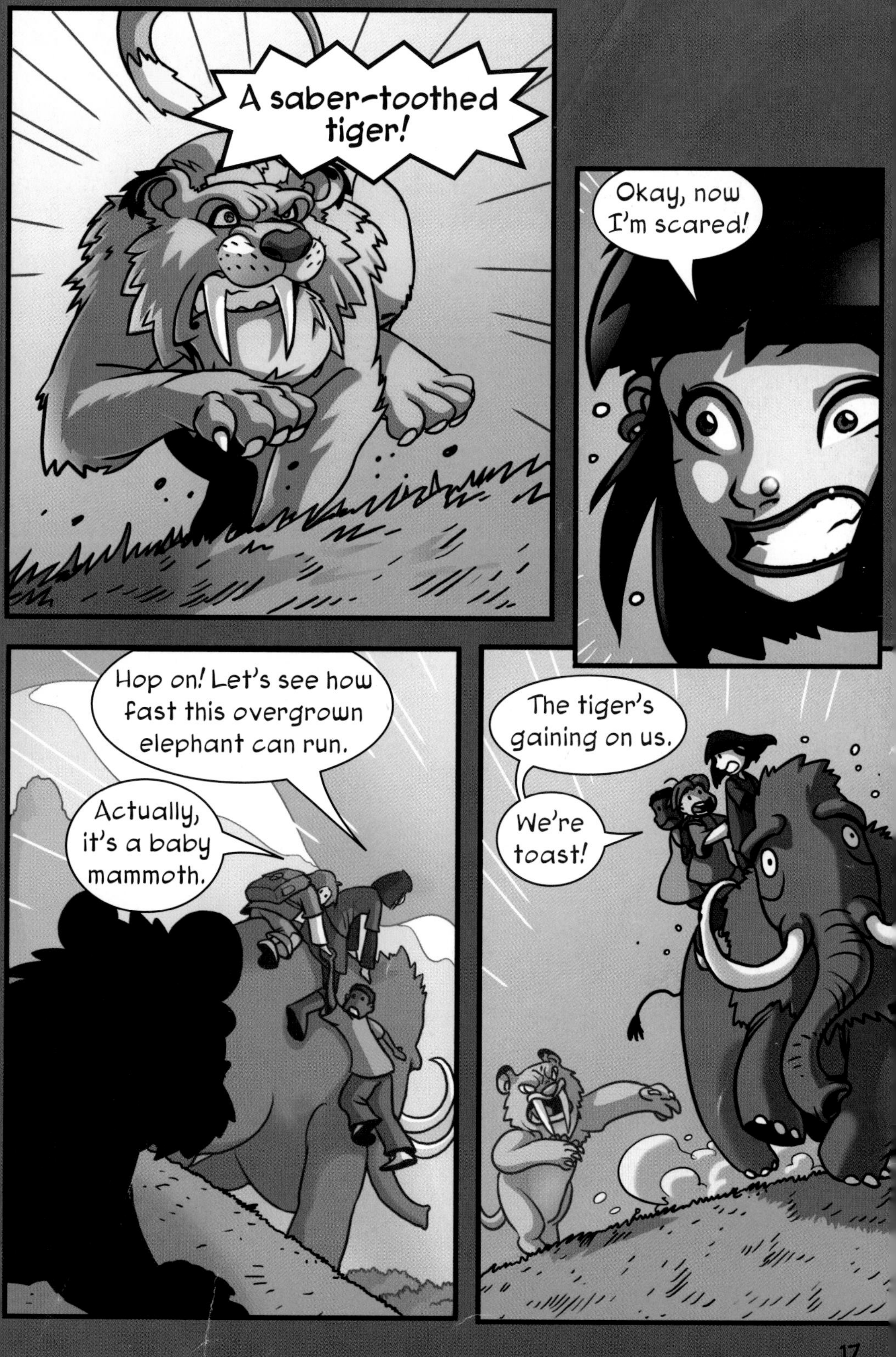
A saber-toothed tiger!
Okay, now I'm scared!
Hop on! Let's see how fast this overgrown elephant can run.
Actually, it's a baby mammoth.
The tiger's gaining on us.
We're toast!

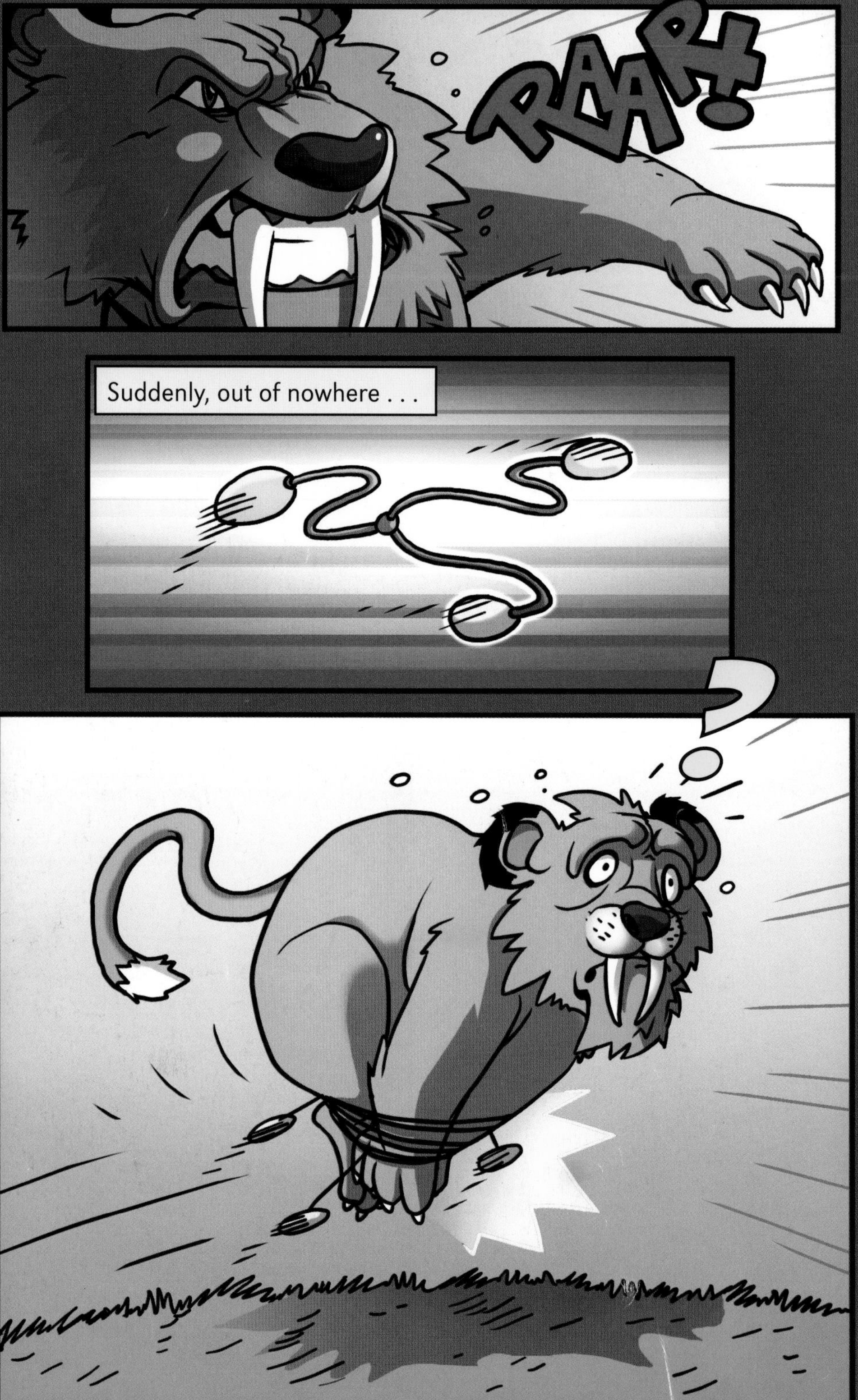
RAAR!
Suddenly, out of nowhere . . .
?

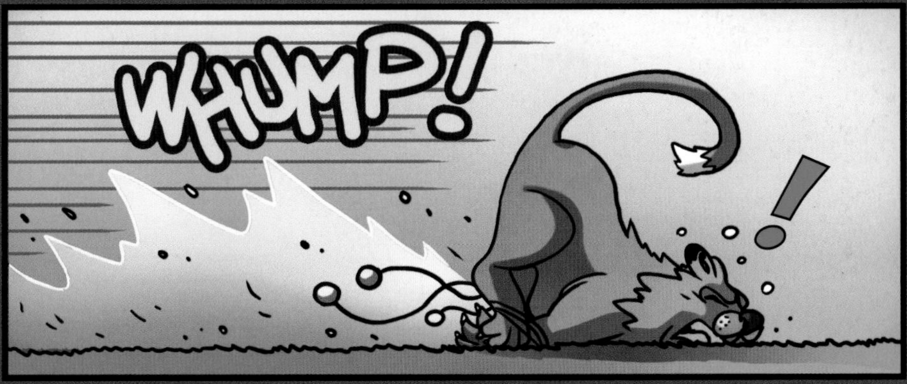
WHUMP!
!

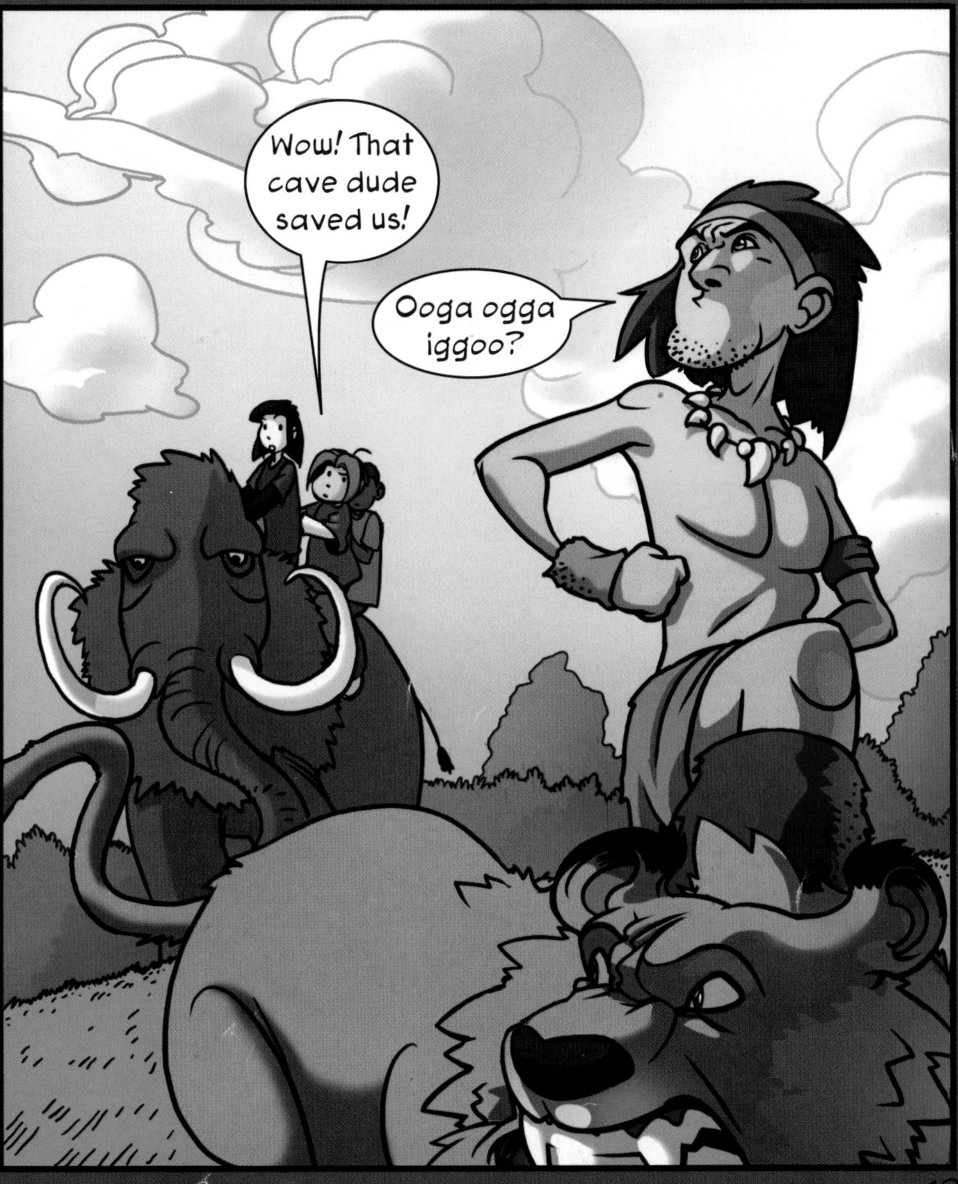
Wow! That cave dude saved us!
Ooga ogga iggoo?

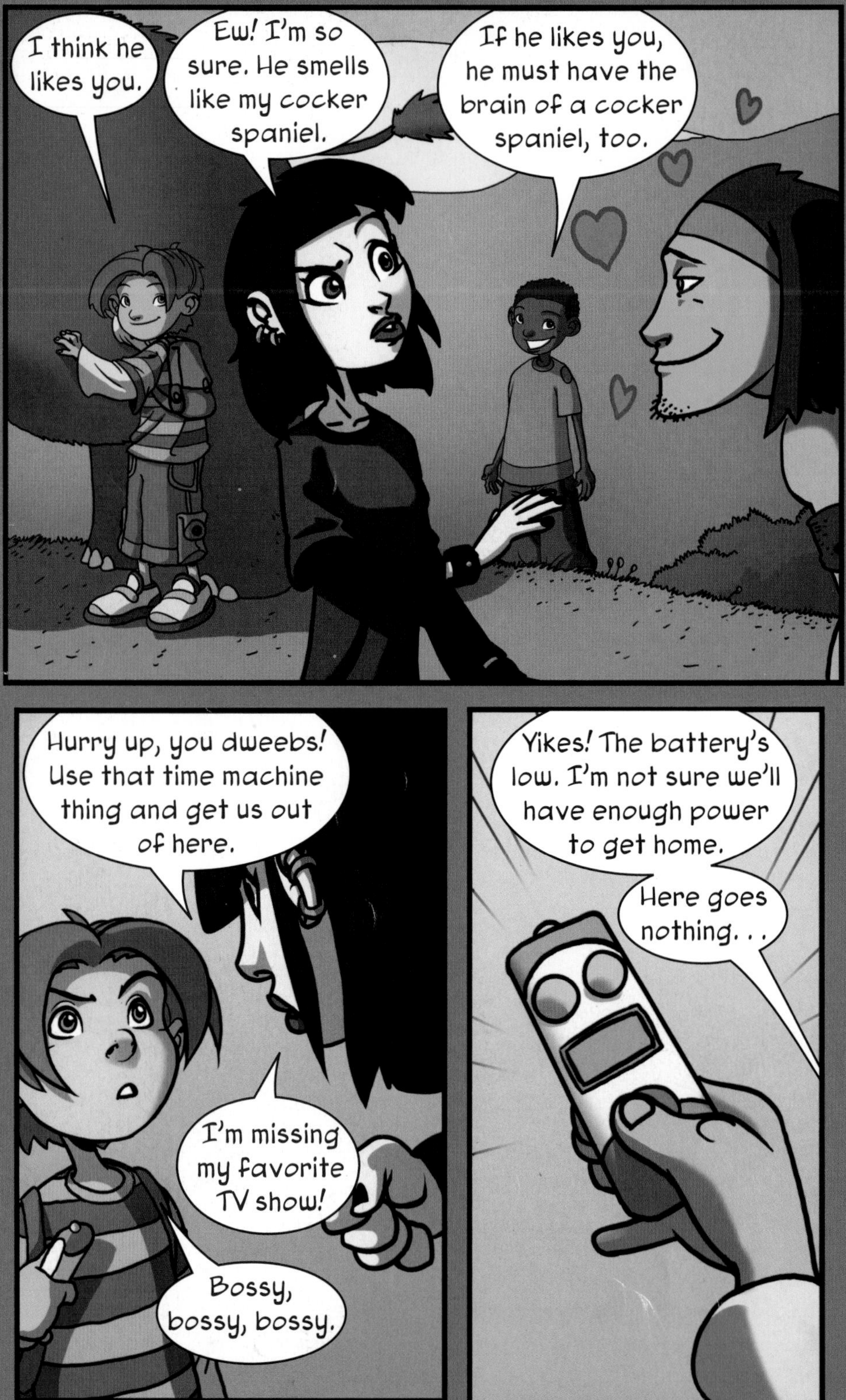
I think he likes you.
Ew! I'm so sure. He smells like my cocker spaniel.
If he likes you, he must have the brain of a cocker spaniel, too.
Hurry up, you dweebs! Use that time machine thing and get us out of here.
I'm missing my favorite TV show!
Bossy, bossy, bossy.
Yikes! The battery's low. I'm not sure we'll have enough power to get home.
Here goes nothing. . .

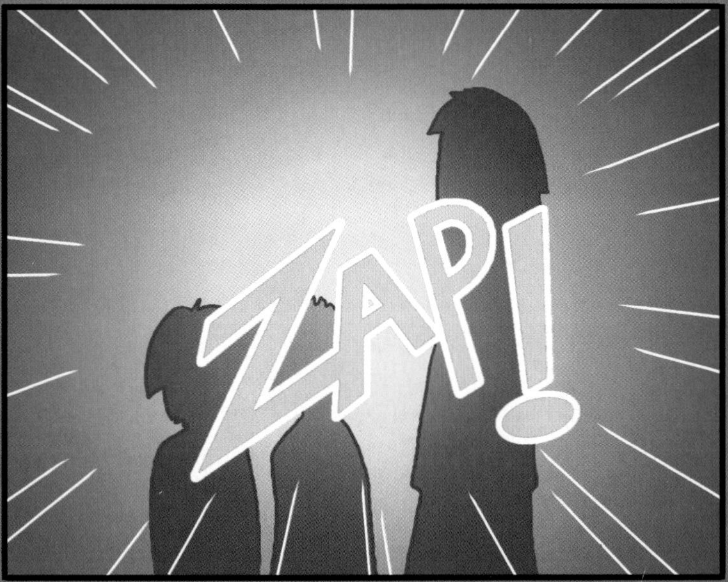
ZAP!

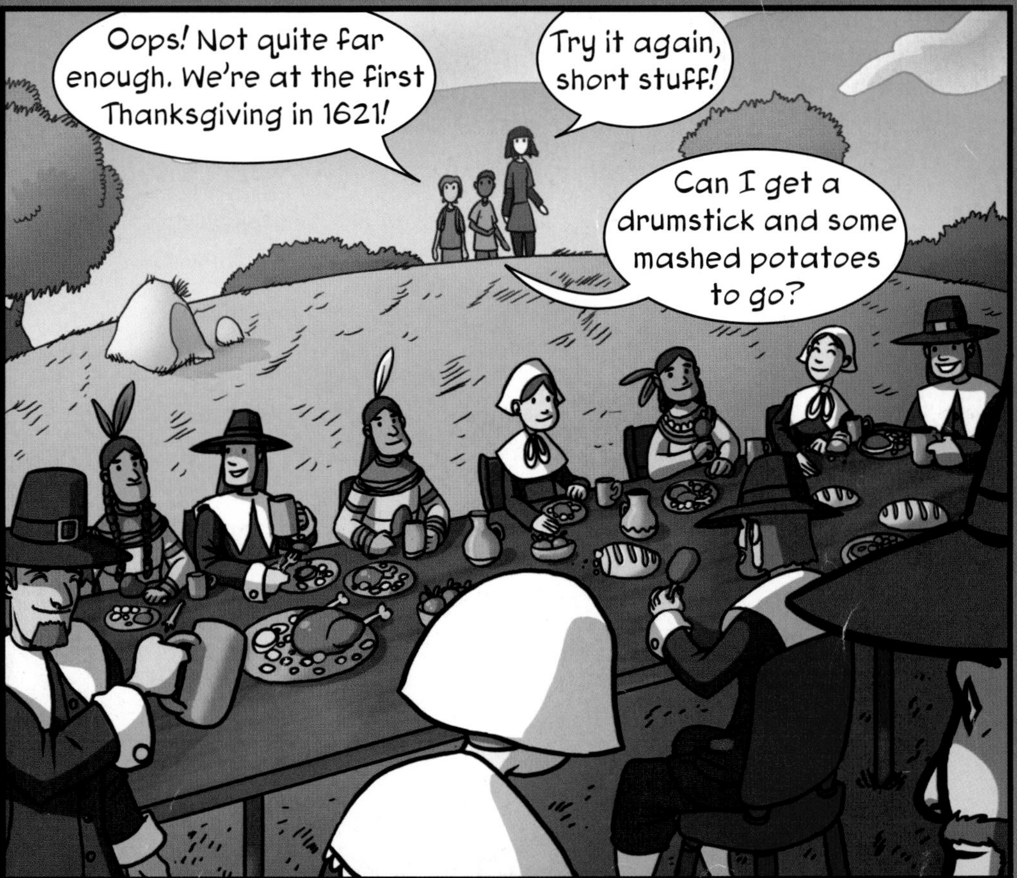
Oops! Not quite far enough. We're at the first Thanksgiving in 1621!
Try it again, short stuff!
Can I get a drumstick and some mashed potatoes to go?

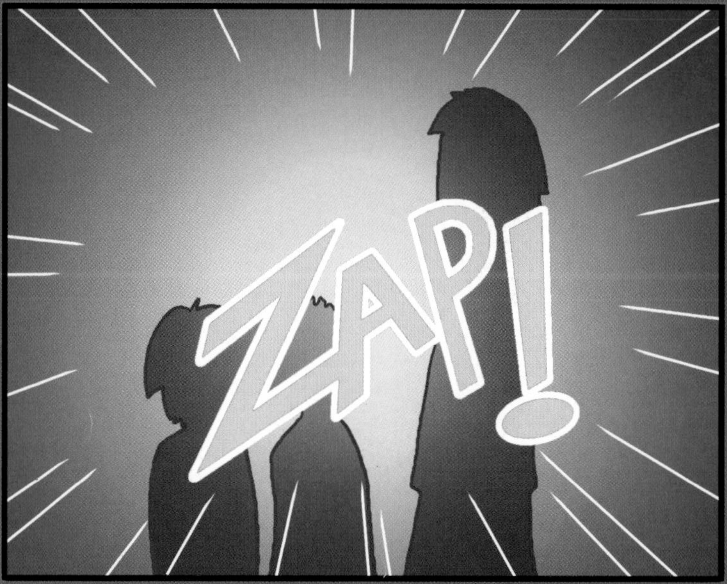
ZAP!

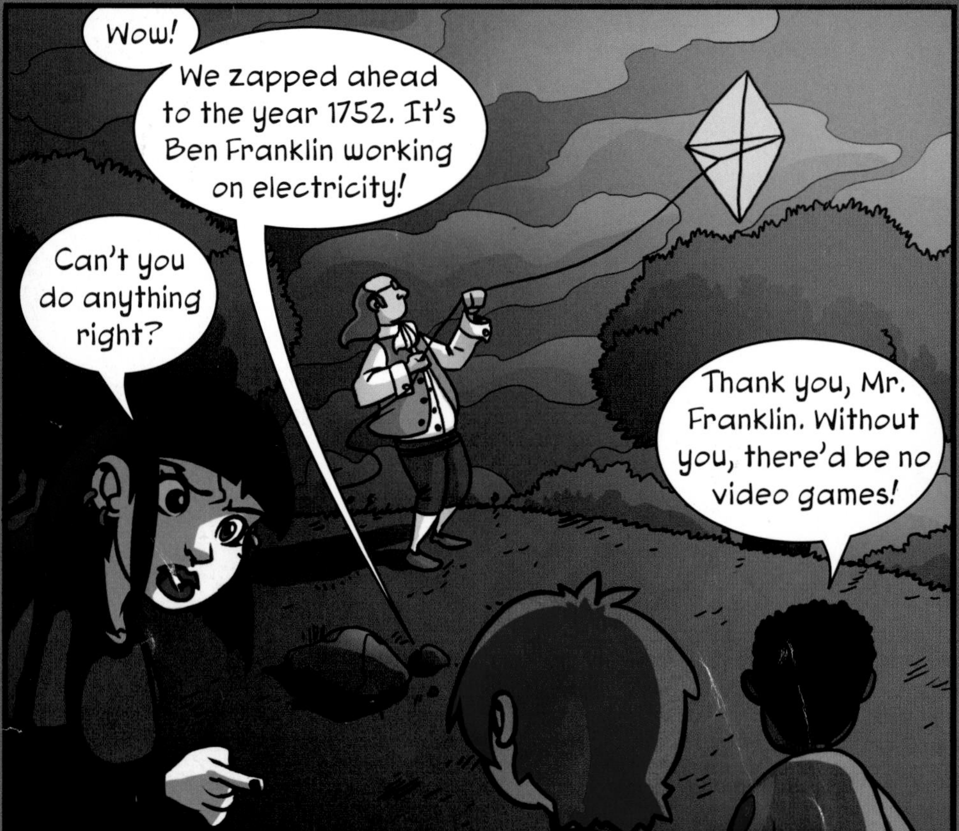
Wow!
We zapped ahead to the year 1752. It's Ben Franklin working on electricity!
Can't you do anything right?
Thank you, Mr. Franklin. Without you, there'd be no video games!

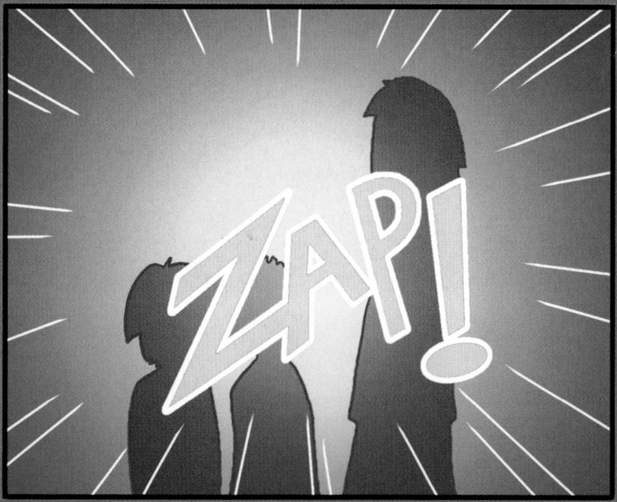
ZAP!

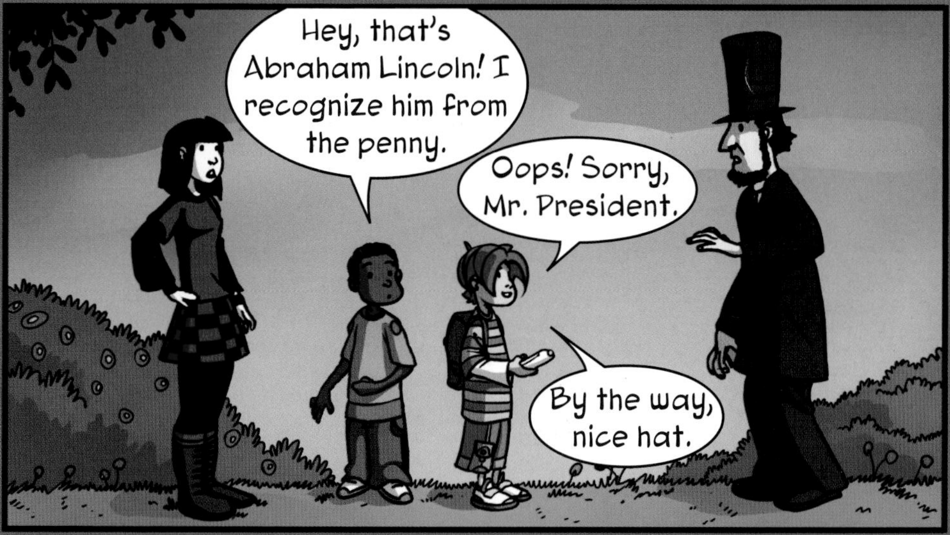
Hey, that's Abraham Lincoln! I recognize him from the penny.
Oops! Sorry, Mr. President.
By the way, nice hat.

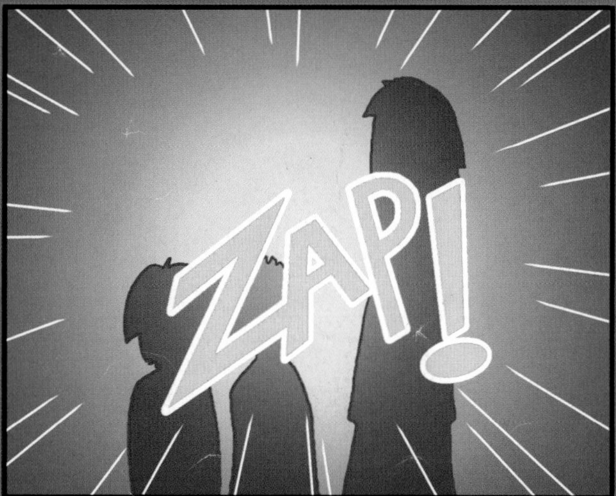
ZAP!

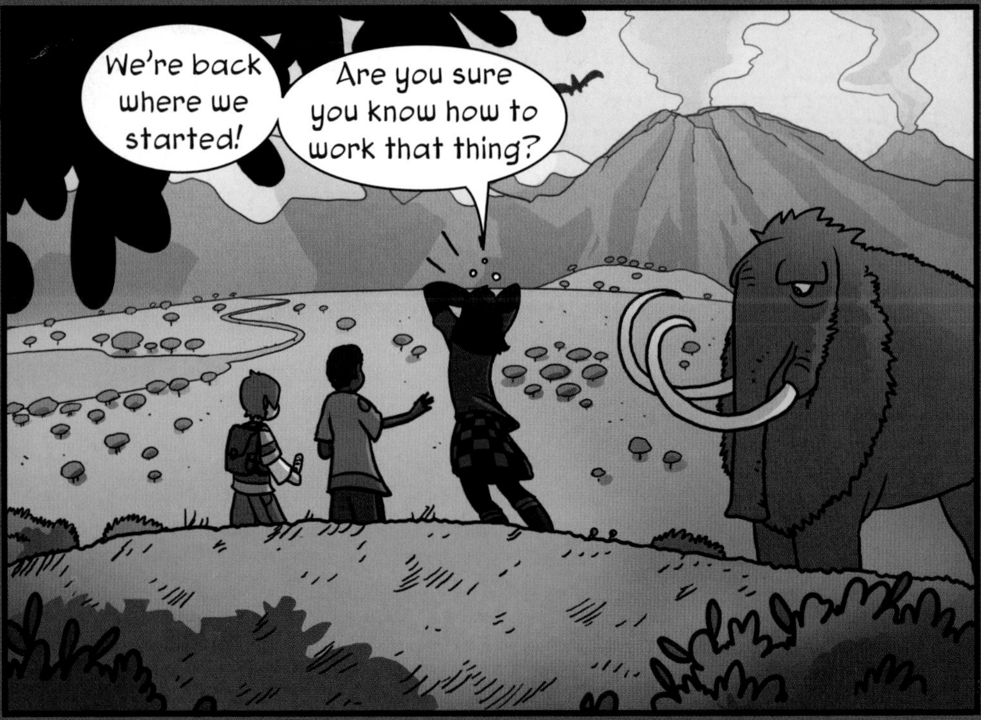
We're back where we started!
Are you sure you know how to work that thing?

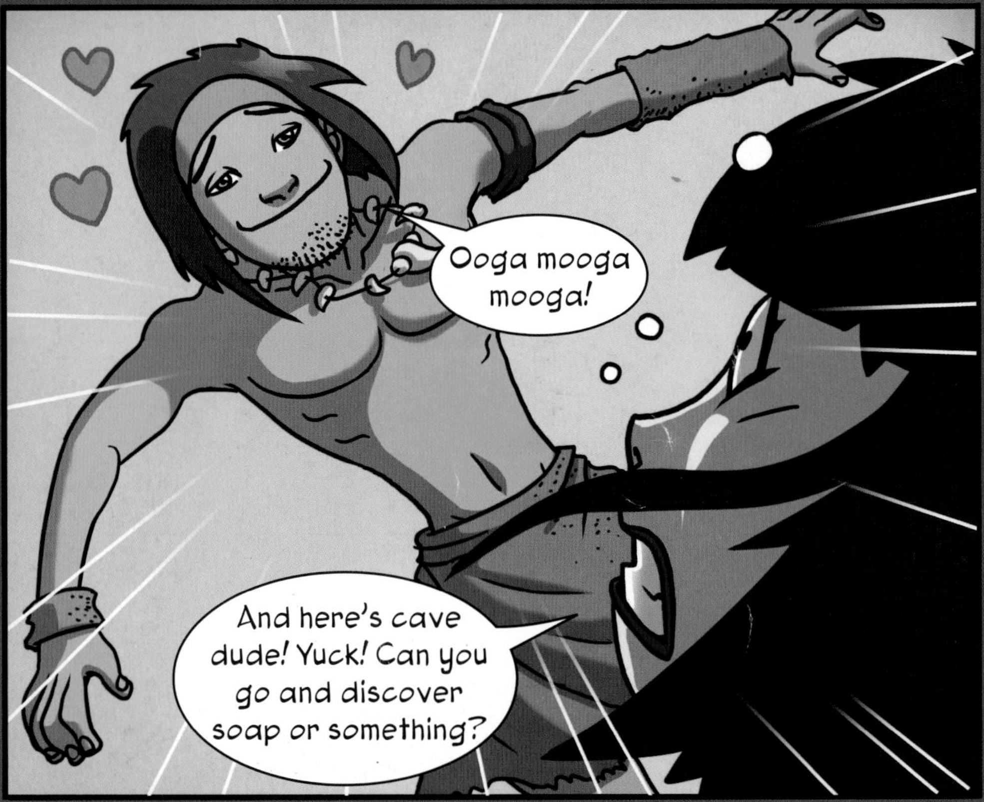
Ooga mooga mooga!
And here's cave dude! Yuck! Can you go and discover soap or something?

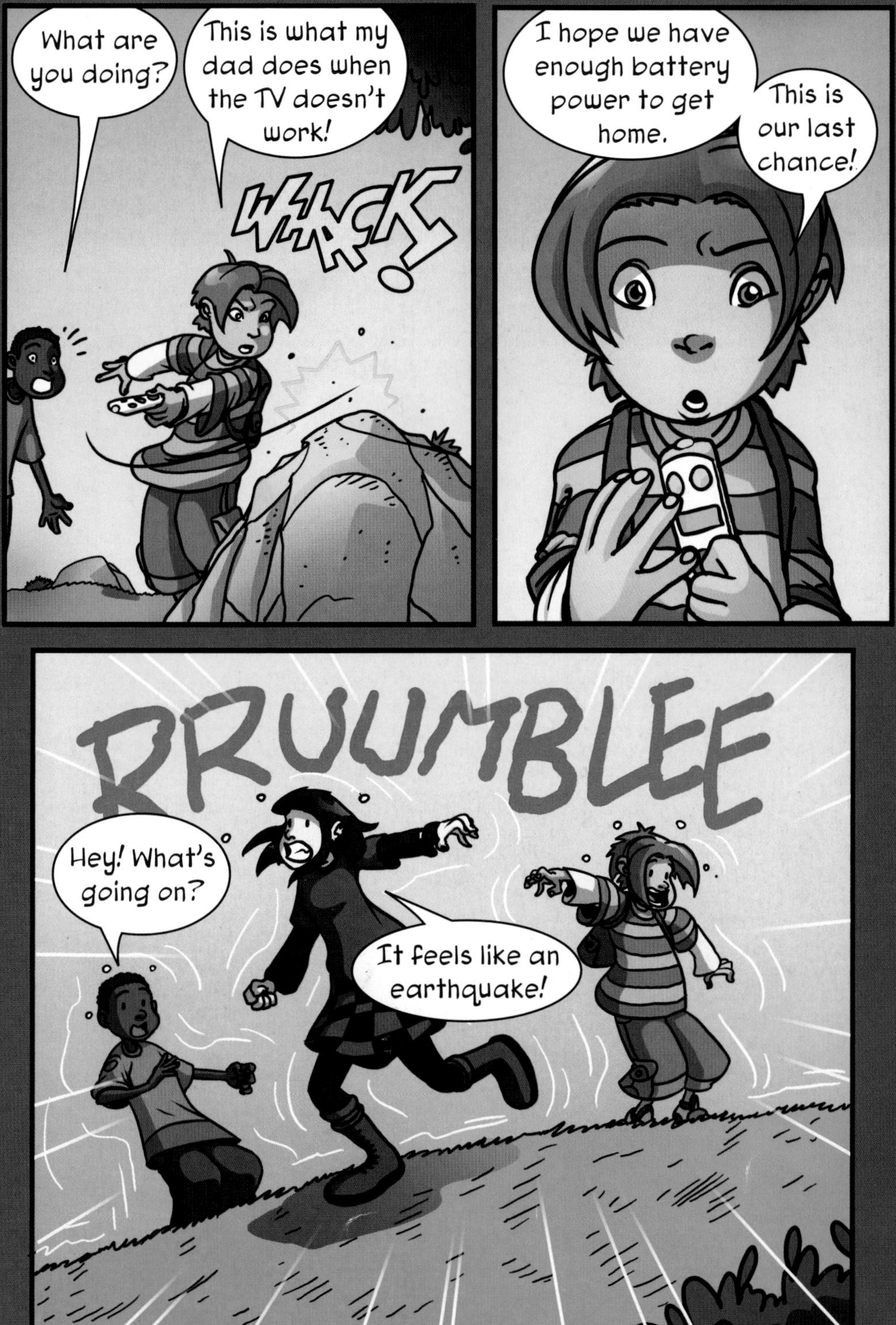
What are you doing?
This is what my dad does when the TV doesn't work!
WHACK!
I hope we have enough battery power to get home.
This is our last chance!
RRUUMBLEE
Hey! What's going on?
It feels like an earthquake!

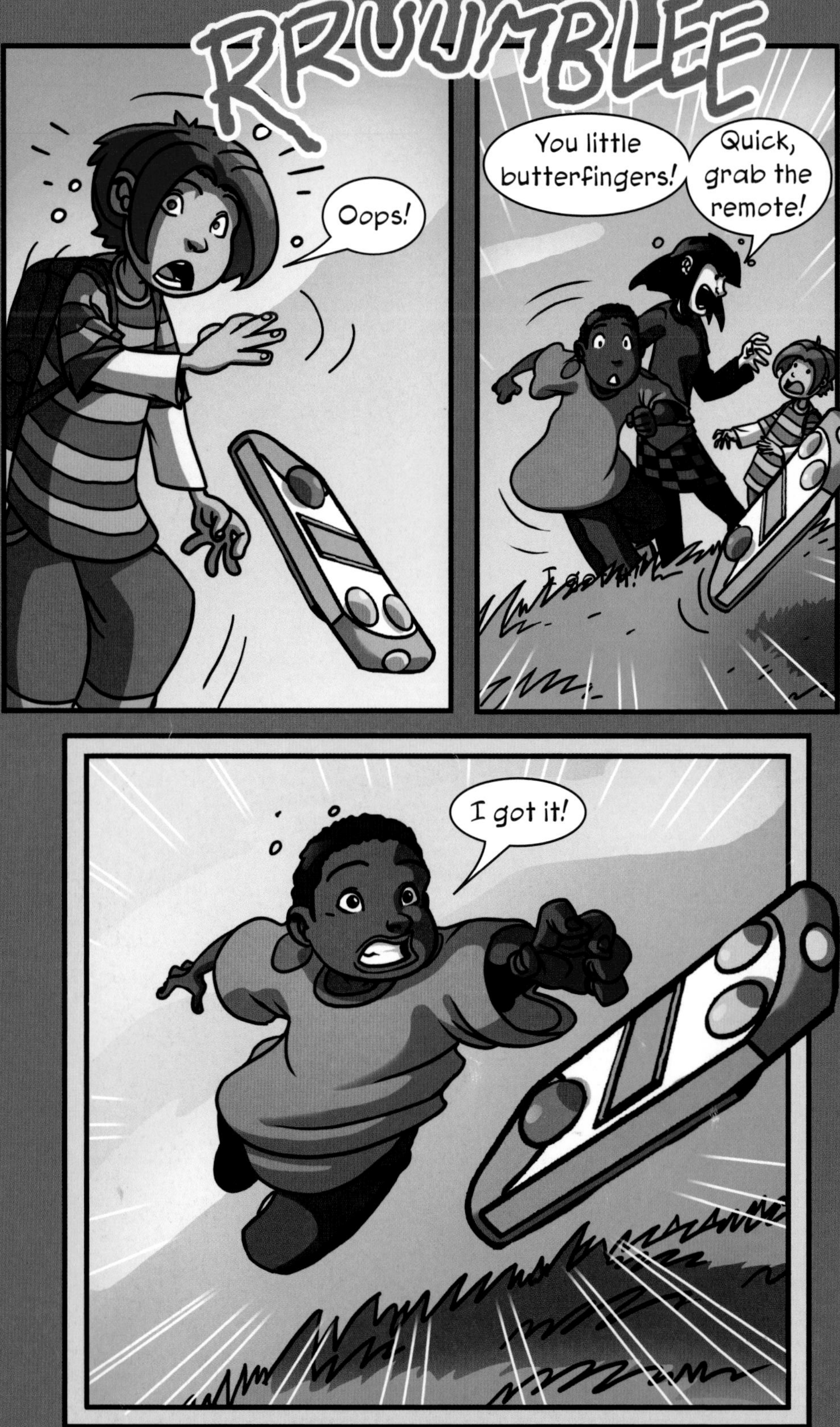
RRUUMBLEE
Oops!
You little butterfingers!
Quick, grab the remote!
I got it!

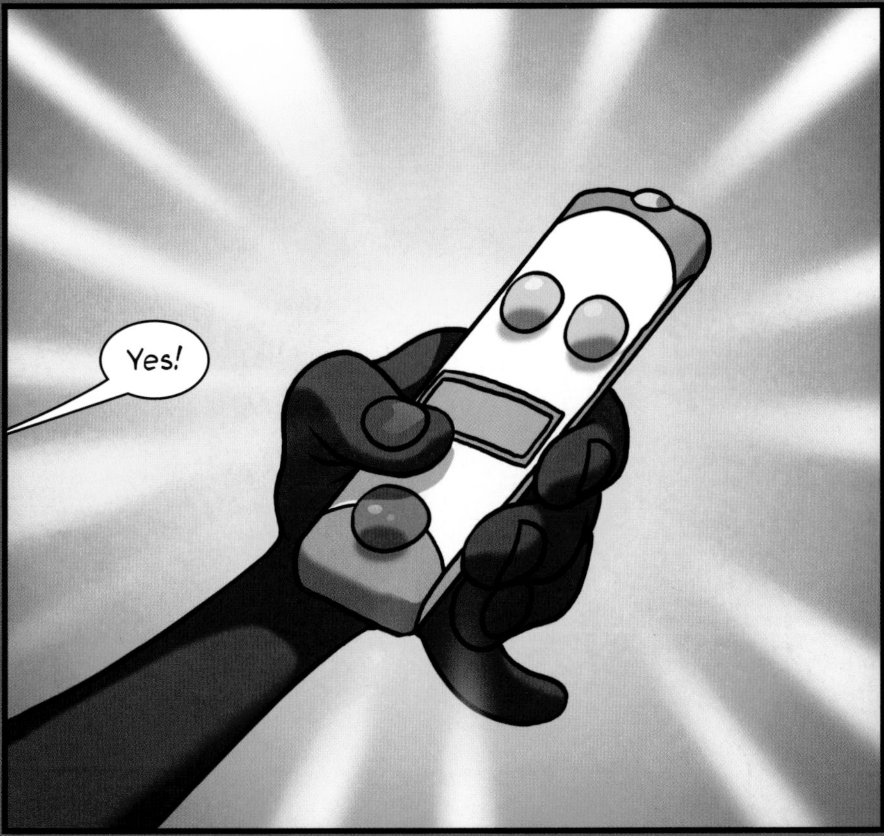
Yes!

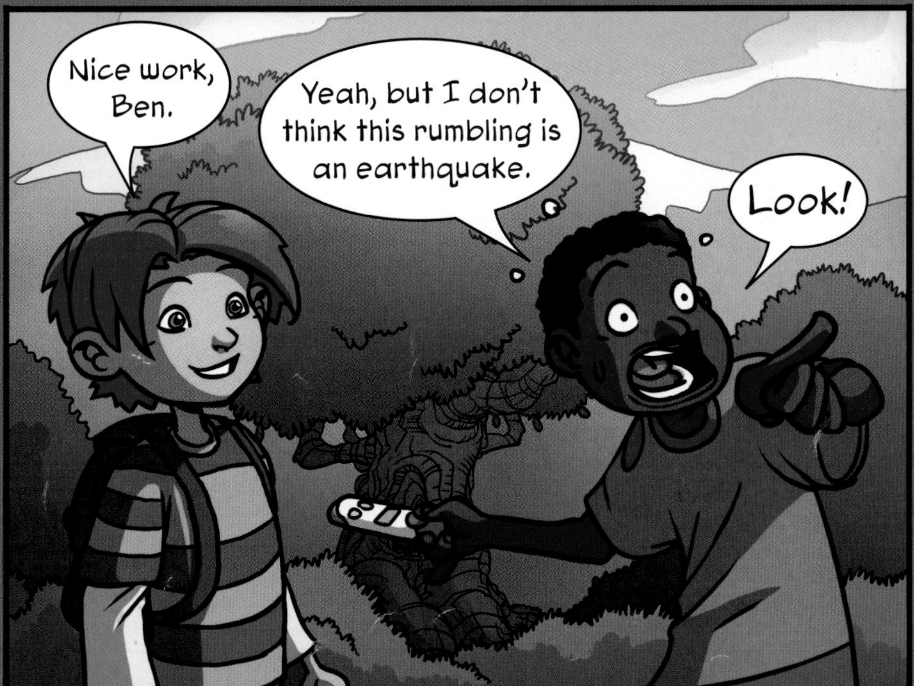
Nice work, Ben.
Yeah, but I don't think this rumbling is an earthquake.
Look!

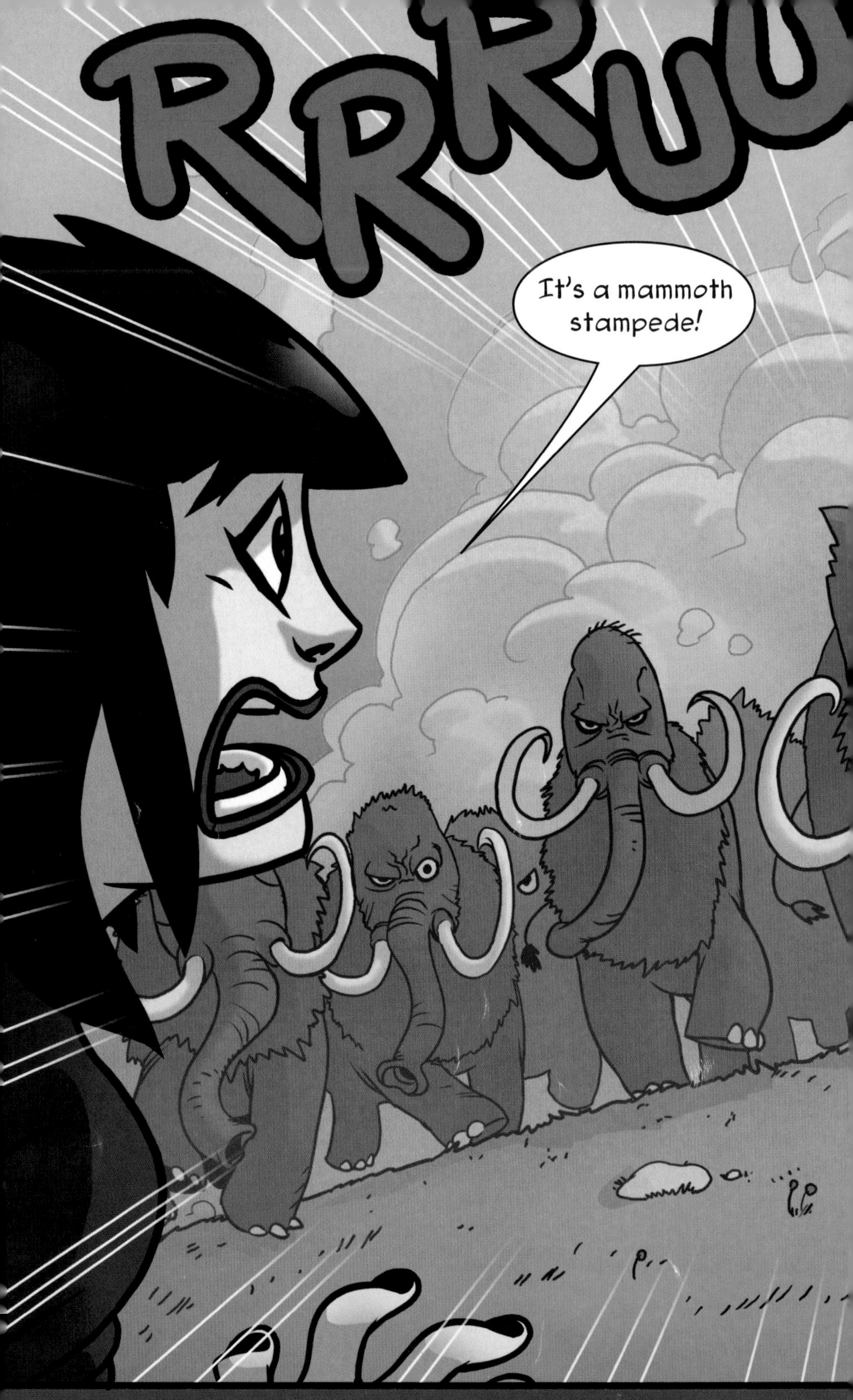
RRKUU
It's a mammoth stampede!

MBLLEE
Unless we want to become prehistoric pancakes, we need to get out of here.
Now!

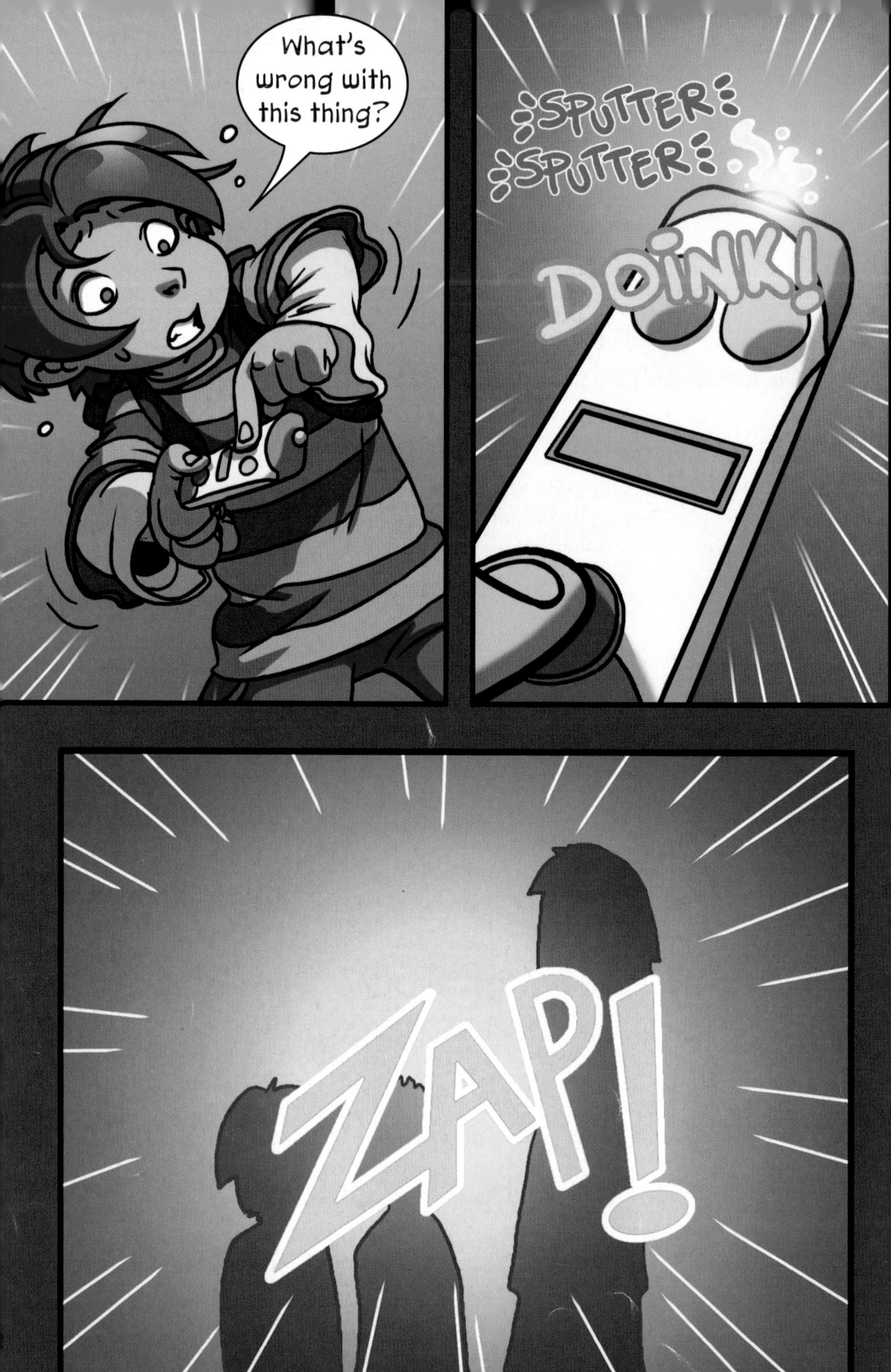
What's wrong with this thing?
SPUTTER
SPUTTER
DOINK!
ZAP!

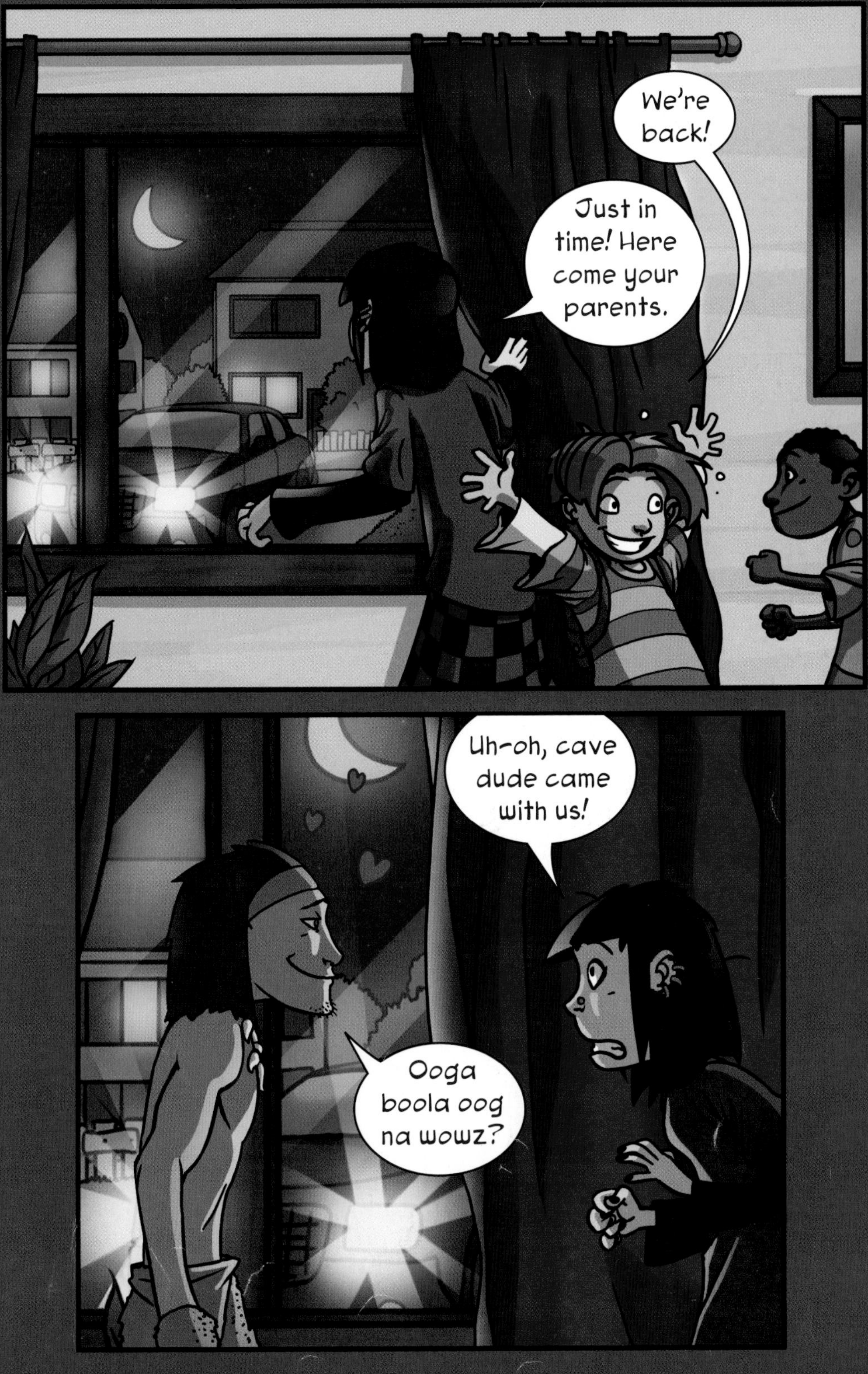
We're back!
Just in time! Here come your parents.
Uh-oh, cave dude came with us!
Ooga boola oog na wowz?

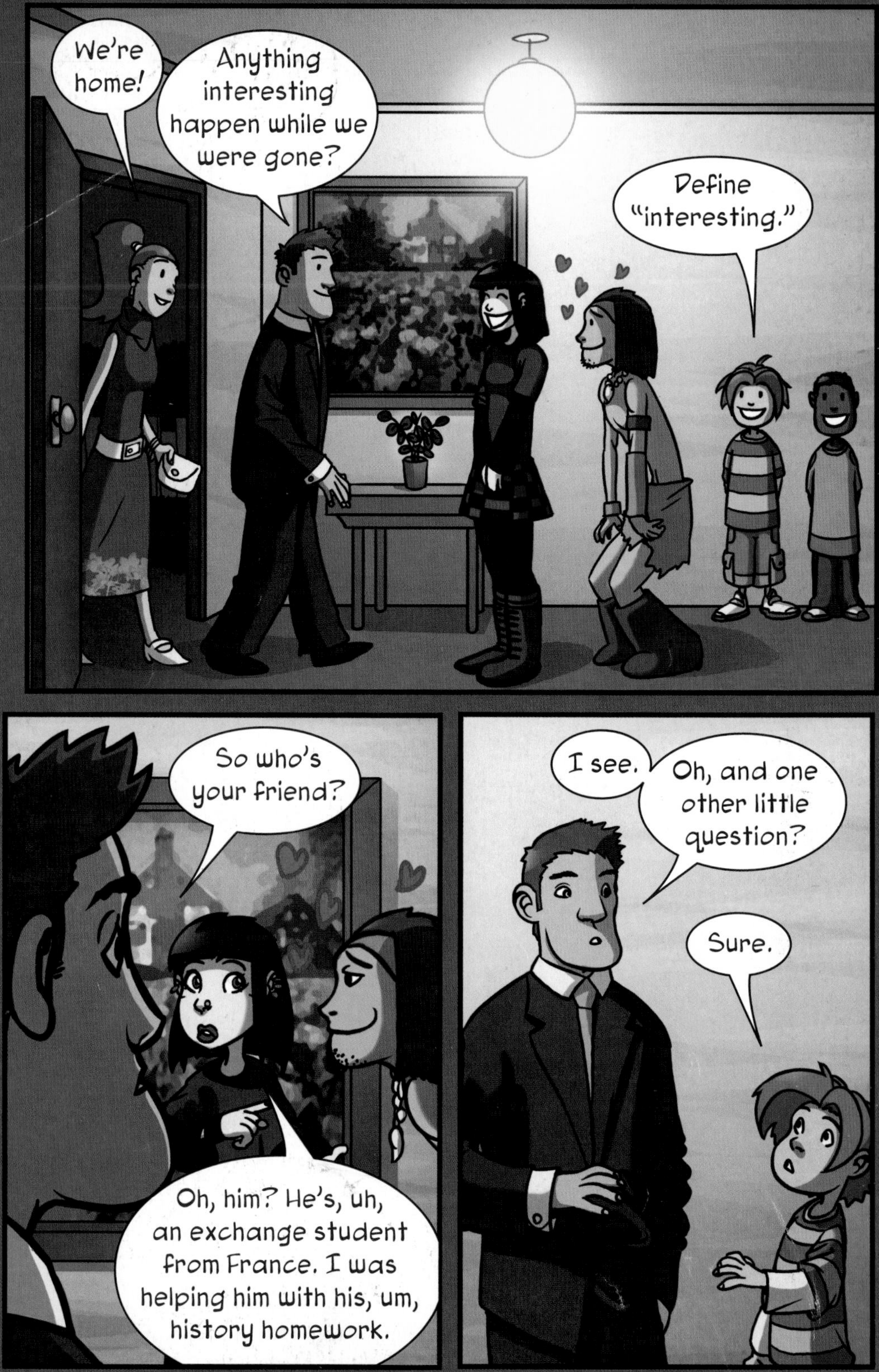
We're home!
Anything interesting happen while we were gone?
Define "interesting."
So who's your friend?
Oh, him? He's, uh, an exchange student from France. I was helping him with his, um, history homework.
I see.
Oh, and one other little question?
Sure.

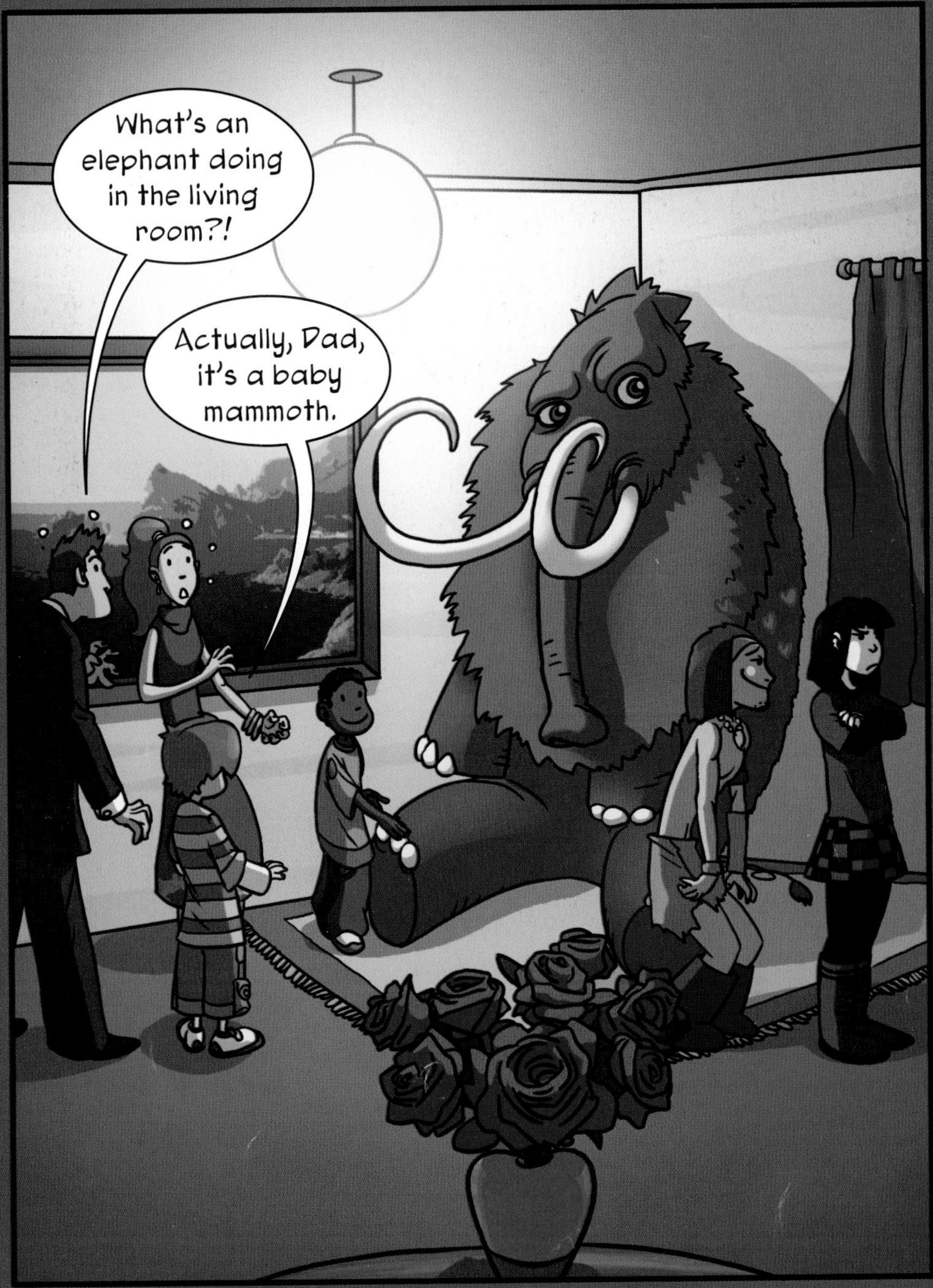
What's an elephant doing in the living room?!
Actually, Dad, it's a baby mammoth.

The end.

ABOUT THE AUTHOR

Growing up, Scott Nickel wanted to be a comic book writer or a mad scientist. As an adult, he gets to do both. In his secret literary lab, Scott has created more than a dozen graphic novels for Stone Arch Books featuring time travel, zombies, robots, giant insects, and mutant lunch ladies. Scott's *Night of the Homework Zombies* received the 2007 Golden Duck award for Best Science Fiction Picture Book. When not creating crazy comics, Scott squeezes in a full-time job as a writer and editor at Jim Davis's Garfield studio. He lives in Muncie, Indiana, with his wife, two teenage sons, and an ever-growing number of cats.

ABOUT THE ILLUSTRATOR

Enrique (ehn-REE-kay) Corts became a professional illustrator at age 19, working on short stories for a Spanish comic magazine. After finishing his art studies, he entered the graphic design and advertising world, spending endless hours chained to his computer. Later, he worked as a concept artist in Great Britain on video games such as *Worms 3D, EyeToy Play 3,* and *Play 4.*

Enrique lives in Palma de Mallorca, Spain. Enrique thinks perhaps someday he will go back to his native Valencia in his quest for more sunlight.

GLOSSARY

butterfingers (BUHT-ur-fing-gurz)—someone who often drops or lets things slip through their hands

exchange student (eks-CHAYNJ STOOD-uhnt)—a person living and studying in another country to experience a different culture

Ice Age (EYESS AYJ)—a period of time in history when ice covered much of Earth

mammoth (MAM-uhth)—an elephant-like animal that lived during the Ice Age and had long tusks and shaggy hair

pip-squeak (PIHP-SKWEEK)—an insulting word referring to an unimportant or small person

prehistoric (pree-hi-STOR-ik)—a time before historical events were written down

rascal (RASS-kuhl)—a tricky, sly person, or a name an older kid might call you

saber-toothed tiger (SAY-bur TOOTHT TYE-gur)—a tiger-like animal that lived during the Ice Age and had long, pointy teeth. Never call a saver-toothed tiger a "pip-squeak"!

MORE ABOUT THE ICE AGE

During the Great Ice Age, sheets of ice more than a mile thick covered much of North America and Europe. And you thought winter was bad! Here are a few more facts about this chilly time in history.

Scientists believe Earth has experienced four major ice ages. The **Great Ice Age** began more than one million years ago and ended just 15,000 years ago.

Large glaciers, or ice sheets, covered nearly one-third of Earth during the Great Ice Age. Even today, some of this ice still hasn't melted in Greenland and Antarctica.

As these huge glaciers grew, they dug out canyons and valleys and pushed up hills and ridges. When the glaciers melted, they left behind many lakes and swamps.

As ocean water froze, sea levels dropped more than 350 feet. Many areas that are now under water would have been dry land. In fact, during the Great Ice Age, Florida was nearly twice as large as it is today.

Many large animals, such as woolly mammoths and saber-toothed tigers, roamed North America during the Great Ice Age. When the ice melted, these animals, also known as **megafauna** (MEG-uh-faw-nuh) became extinct. Today, scientists still discover their fossils.

Temperatures during the Great Ice Age must have been extremely cold, right? Actually, much of Earth was only a few degrees colder than today.

HOW BIG WERE THE ICE SHEETS?

Ocean
Land
Ice Sheet

DISCUSSION QUESTIONS

1. David and Ben didn't like their babysitter, Pamela. So why did they go back in time to save her life? Explain your answer.

2. Each page of a graphic novel has several illustrations called panels. What is your favorite panel in this book? Describe what you like about the illustration and why it's your favorite.

3. What do you think should happen to David? Should he be punished or rewarded for going back in time to save the sitter? Explain your answer.

WRITING PROMPTS

1. In this story, a cave man travels with David and Ben back to the present time. What happens next? Does the cave guy learn to fit in at school? Or do the boys send him back to the Ice Age? Write down your ideas.

2. Mammoths and saber-toothed tigers are both extinct animals. Ask an adult to help you find information about another extinct animal. Describe what the animal looked like, where it lived, and what it ate.

3. Make a list of three things you would pack for a journey back in time. Would you want to show a Pilgrim your computer or play videos game with George Washington? Explain each item you would bring and why?

INTERNET SITES

The book may be over, but the adventure is just beginning.

Do you want to read more about the subjects or ideas in this book? Want to play cool games or watch videos about the authors who write these books? Then go to FactHound. At *www.facthound.com*, you'll be able to do all that, and more. The FactHound website can also send you to other safe Internet sites.

Check it out!